Whistle Wood,

Land of the Fathers.

by P. J. Naughton

www.siliconpool.com

Published by www.siliconpool.com

ISBN 978-1-291-25042-8

Printed and bound in the United Kingdom by www.lulu.com

For Kathy and all our children...

This place we live in, this land we call home, has changed now. For generations it hardly changed at all. Now it has changed forever. I was lucky enough to spend my childhood in a place where there was a deep understanding of the countryside and the ways of country folk. Times have changed now. Since my early years this region, in common with most places in England, has changed beyond all recognition. The speed of this change has been truly phenomenal. In the last forty years or so, the traditions and values handed down over centuries have all but disappeared. The aim of this work is to record something of the old ways for posterity, so that some knowledge of traditional values might be savoured by those who wish to read about them. Hopefully this writing will provide a snapshot of how things used to be and provide an insight into how things could have been today, had we done more to preserve our heritage.

Contents

Introduction.

This is the story of my childhood home, the place where I was born and brought up. It is the story of the imaginary village of Whistle Wood. I was born in a village like this in the late fifties and grew up there through out the sixties and seventies. Whistle Wood is part of a cluster of villages, a tightly knit community located on a small Isle of some fifty thousand acres or so, of mostly arable land. It lies in the North of the county of Lincolnshire in the North East Midlands of England. The place has gone now, at least the place that it was. For scores of years, stretching way back into antiquity, it had remained almost unchanged. I was lucky, I was born just in time to catch a glimpse of the way it had always been.

Since my early years Whistle Wood has changed beyond recognition. I feel it's important to record the way it was, whilst someone can still remember it. You might wonder why it should matter. To me that's a bit like asking if polar bears matter. They matter to polar bears and the people who know them and if we only decide they matter after they are gone, then it's just too late. The truth is I felt it was important to record my memories for others to enjoy.

At first sight it might appear to be an ordinary kind of place and in many ways it was and still is. But in so many ways being ordinary is very different now. All the more reason why I felt something of it had to be preserved. Life was more certain in those times.

Nature was so well known, more lived in, more acknowledged, more understood. It's generally thought we move forward in all areas, as time goes by. This was certainly the feeling back then. But certainly less is known now about much that was far better known in previous times. This is the sad truth. It's probably been the case now for quite some time. As science finds out more, more people seem less concerned with the need to know, unless for some reason they suddenly find they need to. Why learn when you can just look it all up when required? Overall we probably have access to more knowledge than ever before in our history but at the same time we probably have the lowest desire to learn. The saddest truth is that looking something up is no real substitute for genuinely understanding something. The people of these parts seemed to understand this very well in the old days.

The area I am talking about certainly played some small part in history and it might have been this understanding which helped the people to recognise what was important. It was from these parts, in the early seventeenth century, that several people from nearby villages, tired of relentless religious persecution, decided to leave in search of a better life overseas. Several locals became members of the very first group of Pilgrim Fathers who eventually set sail from Plymouth to the New World on 16th September 1620. It is difficult to imagine the courage this must have taken – to leave for an unknown world, to navigate such a massive expanse of sea and survive on their own, totally unaided, save for the efforts and endeavours of the people in their immediate group. What a challenge. It's hard to imagine a situation that would require the same sort of courage today.

Amongst the Founding Fathers was one William Bradford who played a major role in the early lives of the first Pilgrims. William was born close to the Isle in the nearby village of Austerfield. He became the architect and second signatory of the Mayflower Compact and was the man who proclaimed the first 'Thanksgiving'. In their first Winter, about half the colonists perished, amongst them was their first leader, John Carver. William was elected as the second leader after John Carver died and in total he served fifteen "two year" terms as Governor of the Plymouth Colony in Massachusetts. What memories must he have taken with him of his early years back home in England?

The Isle, an inland island surrounded by drainage canals and dykes, was first drained and reclaimed from marshland by Dutch engineer Cornelius Vermuyden in the seventeenth century, only a few years after the first Pilgrim Fathers first set sail on their courageous endeavour.

Indeed it was the drainage work of Vermuyden and his creation of dykes and drainage channels that actually gave form to the Isle as it stands today. The astonishing engineering achievements of Vermuyden were not universally acclaimed at the time, for it robbed many locals of their livelihoods as they relied on the marshland for hunting and fishing. But the drainage transformed the region, converting the rich land for use in highly productive, arable agriculture.

Early in the eighteenth century, this same Isle became the birth place to John and Charles Wesley; religious leaders, philosophers and leading thinkers of their time. These were men with vision, destined for greatness, whose work still impacts on the thoughts and beliefs of millions throughout the world today.

After Vermuyden had completely the astonishing feat of draining the marshland, much of the land on the Isle was available for any one who cleared it of trees and scrub, to claim ownership of it. Whistle Wood was largely covered in dense forest. As such it was one of the last parts of the Isle to be cleared. It is the 'Llareggub' of North Lincolnshire.

Come! I'll show you how things used to be. They say time and tide wait for no man but they certainly took their time in this place and I'm grateful they did, because it gave those of us lucky enough to live there, a chance to glimpse the values and traditions of distant times which had long since been lost in many other areas.

You might think it's impossible to go back in time. Maybe it is. But find somewhere where time has passed more slowly and there you can catch a glimpse of how things used to be. It might not be how your ancestors lived or even how the ancestors of your ancestors lived but rest assured somebody lived there.

I'll take you up hill and down dale. I'll take you behind closed doors. Within a few hours you could know this place like you've lived here for years. Better than you'd see it by just visiting. Sit back, relax. Enjoy the ride. Let the years drift back. Let me take you back to those spirited, happy days of youth and innocence.

None of the people mentioned in this book are real people. They are all fictional characters, invented to portray the nature of the Isle as it was when I was a child. They have been invented to portray the traits and behaviour of people of those times. Perhaps from this you will enjoy a glimpse of how people lived and worked, in those days of innocence.

Empty your mind. Let it be filled with the pictures I paint for you with these simple words. I wrote them in the hope you might enjoy them.

Whistle Wood

P.J. Naughton

1. Welcome To Strawberry Isle.

Travel east for about six miles directly along the great Toffee road from Toffee Town, until you come to a crossing. Pass the 'Travellers Rest' Tavern – you'll know the place easily enough, it's the one with a sign outside announcing, 'No Travellers.' Eventually you'll come to the 'Blue Bell' crossroads. Keep going straight on.

As soon as you cross these crossroads, you'll feel an immediate change. The light is suddenly different, the dykes are blacker and wetter in Winter, the cold cuts deeper. In Spring the air is more fragrant than anywhere else, the blossom hangs thick like velvet. This is far from being the prettiest place in the world but to me the flowers are prettier here in Summer than in any other place I've ever seen. Maybe it's because it's my home; the place where I was born. The birds always sing more tuneful here. In Autumn the berries are sweeter. They glow like berries you have never seen.

Carry on east for another six miles. The road is long and straight, as straight as any Roman road even though it's been walked by all the generations since. It had to have been, it's the only way onto the Isle coming from the West.

You'll pass through a prairie landscape – it's as flat as a pancake. You're heading for New Holland. Until Vermuyden had drained these lands it had been largely bog and marshland. What he created here was a wonderfully fertile plain. Carry on through these Biblical lands, home to some of the Pilgrims; home to many saints and many sinners. Eventually, as you come to the end of this long straight highway, you'll see before you 'the only hill in Lincolnshire.' As soon as you cross a small bridge over a small drain, you'll be on the Isle – and in front of you the hill will open out wide. Welcome to 'Strawberry Isle.' Welcome to 'Whistle Wood.'

Few here remaining have tasted State-side air or Honesdale rain, or seen mountain after mountain or heard the howl of wolves or the growl of mother bears, or felt the buzz of New York.

They'd never care for town living, all those used toilets and trains full of bad breath. It's said that many of the elderly folk have never ventured much beyond the Isle, save for rare visits to one of the nearby towns and even then, only when they absolutely had to. But in this place you become aware of your context, the fact that you are sharing, sharing the land and sharing breath, not only with all the other people, from the very old to the very newest born, from those dying and those about to give birth but also with all the animals of the forests and farms and fields; the pigs, the cows, the horses, the goats, the foxes and hares, the birds and the butterflies, the bees and the worms.

This is a special place. And like any other special place it has undeniable qualities but it also has its very own imperfections. For example, it is the kind of place where men have to mix the beers in the pub, stout and bitter, black and tan, trying to create an ale that can be consumed. It's a place of survival where dogs will happily respond to two or more names and will follow children home in the hope of cadging a boiled potato.

Whistle Wood

It's a place where old men sit outside their front doors on kitchen chairs whilst their wives sit beside them in hand knitted cardigans, peeling potatoes into washing up bowls. It's a place where tin foil from 'meat and potato' pies from the pub are tied to string to frighten geese off the vegetables growing in the garden - the same geese that hiss and make good gravy, the same geese that provide grease for rubbing on bad chests and provide soft feathers for stuffing the softest pillows.

This is the time when windows are single glazed, this is the time before central heating has been heard of, when frost forms on the insides of windows during cold nights, when houses generally only have one fire, a fire made of coal, that takes far longer to light than it takes people to dress in the pale shivering light of it's feeble firelighter flame.

This is the time when many schools and homes still have outside lavatories, it's a time when the Dilly cart still has to come to empty them, none too soon at the end of every stinking fortnight. It's a time when children still wave at steam trains from banks of buttercup and bluebells, when children spend weeks collecting wood for Bonfire night and enjoy homemade treacle toffee crafted by old ladies, competing to make the thickest, blackest, strongest, richest, most solid treacle sweetest sweetness. On this, the night of Guy Fawkes, sparks will sparkle in children's hands and eyes and up across the black murky shuddering ferment of the deep, black, endless sky.

This is the time when chips are cooked in pans of sizzling boiling pork fat, often on open fires. Flat, sliced potato chips with faces cut into them, the flavour, the smoke, dripping in tomato sauce; dripping in dripping; dripping on bread, dripping in butter. Old men eat soup, straining the bits through their moustaches - soup for breakfast, lunch and tea, often out of the same tin with only a few slices of bread with each meal. Old women soak raw tripe in milk for hours and slip it into their mouths past their naked gums with trembling anticipation.

This is the time when the land is still full of flowers - wild flowers. Flowers that stand strong and bright in full spectral arcs across the fertile lands — even in the glittering spangled quartz sands of the East and in the warp land and black land where coal breaks through to the surface.

For the only force ranged against nature is the sweat and toil and labour of the young men and despite the considerable might ranged against her, nature still just holds the upper hand.

This is the time when fish fill the rivers in huge swarms, when strawberries fill the fields with the smell of their glowing fruit, when farmers' wives trade eggs and home made butter and work the patchwork of fields. It is a time of village shoots, a time of plump wild pigeons and woodcock and pot roasts, a time when nature and life and abundance never seem to know any end.

This land is teaming with life, wild beast and plants of so many different forms. Not one square inch of soil is wasted, not one flower, not one drip of honey, not even from one wild bee. It is a time of honey and sweet blossom, laidened orchards, baskets and baskets of fruit, potatoes and sweet corn, celery and herbs.

This is a town of beer and tobacco smoke, cigarettes, pipes and cigars, a crazy town, an ordinary town, but alas, a town unlike any other. Lulu sings crackling from the open windows of passing vans.

Caged ferrets pace and gaze from the homes of these country folk; folk who know how to dress a wild rabbit for the pot and survive and flourish where other lesser folk would surely perish.

Old men sit, apparently not talking, shaking their heads in despair or nodding in agreement. Rich twists of tobacco from far off lands are rubbed and fed gently into their ancient smoking pipes. Guns are cleaned and polished. Gunpowder and lead-shot are groomed and fed into cartridges and stowed carefully in readiness. Fugitive foxes are out stealing and stalking the hopelessly bright coloured pheasants who are blissfully unaware of the striking flash of colour which betrays their presence. The fox fears the gun but the pheasant must fear the fox and the gun and yet somehow both survive in abundance, in some kind of natural balance, despite the obvious difference in their instincts and standing in the wilds.

This day is a May day. If ever time comes to a halting full stop, let us hope it happens on a bright May day, so that we might enjoy one of the very best days of the year throughout eternity. Above any other, this month offers such promise.

There's lilac if you are lucky and sweet fragrant apple blossom. Succulent moist buds adorn the verdant trees and bushes and there's even the promise of roses. May flowers glow white with feints of pink, marsh marigolds linger and shine brighter than gold. Bluebells mirror the echo of the dawn and the skies fill with swallows.

Old Woman 1:

"In May he sings all day."

This is the time when cuckoos sing from every possible woodland glade. Enjoy this annual choral festival whilst you can. In June he'll change his tune, in July he'll get ready to fly.

This is the glow of dawn - both shades of dawn. Watch carefully! As slow as time itself, each day begins with its very own miracle. Listen. Listen as slow as time itself. Watch carefully. Watch slowly. Blossom more beautiful than anything else on Earth, shivers silently in the hedgerows. Somehow the sparkling drops of dew remain unmoved. See the violets as they start to unfurl their magic. Roses too will appear, having readied themselves through the darkness of the night.

On this sparkling dawn people are preparing for turning the land upon which we all rely. Dealing with the weather brings challenges throughout the year. How quickly the bitter piercing frost, two pairs of socks and tin foil in Wellington boots against the leaks and thick wet mud, turn into the blazing, relentless fire of the concrete sun baked, blistering sun. The frozen iron ground melts so quickly into mud and dries to dust. But this is May, the favourite in between time - moderate weather with welcome gentle sunlight and yet with the promise of warmer, drier days to come.

Even now there is sadness. When the last blossom falls from the trees, when the last tears of Winter fall, when the sun warms the Earth. Even with so much promise, when fragrance and light emerge from the cold, dark frozen Winter, there is a sense of passing. But for now we can enjoy the beauty for this day, if no other, we will live for this day alone.

As we come into the village, we pass the first farm, just across from Monkham bridge. It's barely light. In the morning forest, amongst the frozen thorn, deep in the forest wastelands of the cold and hungry dawn, dazed and drunken, each night speaks with its own language.

Here we see Squire 'Barley' Green milking as he has done every morning for so many years. As he works away in turn at the udders and at his cows, Barley whispers sweet poetry to his herd.

Barley:

"Violets scent this dawn. May the cloak of darkness sweep gently and rub darkness from our eyes. Distant churchyards chime from somewhere distant 'cross the hill. By those same chimes this day is born, dressed ready to meet the touch of dawn, the fruits of nature's silence shine.

Cock crows wake the whistled forest, the miracle of a day begun, the buzz of dawn, the glow of warmth, the waking blossom showers fragrance. Nectared mist sips the sweetest bloom. A riot of rainbow colour, blossoms in hedgerows, amongst them the precious violet. The magic of the bloom of dawn, witnessed daily, every morn, in hedgerow 'cross this land.

Deep in the forest, from the purple of the night, the gift of marriage of dew and seed, sown by the breeze of the random wild by chance of nature or by thirst of rain, if by chance to be taken by the hand of child, to mark one mother's beauty. The magic gilded hue, at the very touch of dawn; the very fruit of forest wombs.

Warm eggs sway aloft, high in our cathedral trees. The midnight violet yearns for light throughout the shades of dawn. When I think of what I was and what I have become.

The witnessed miracle, the page is turned, the world moves on. Midnight moves far off now, throughout some distant wood. In the churchyard chime that signalled, the passing of another day.
In that very chime, a new beginning, for we are never left for one moment, without a day.

And so the endless thirst for life and rain, the light of life, the touch of night, my words will stand without my breath."

The cows munch in blissful, chewing disregard for Barley and his words but he is convinced it helps with the yield and with the fat content and the butter-churn. In common with nearly every farmer in this village, Barley is very proud of his own farm. Farms are more than places of work, they are showcases of a life's endeavour.

Competition is fierce to maintain the very highest standards of appearance. Gates are whitewashed, yards are swept, hedges are neatly trimmed, lawns are always freshly cut. A large oak barrel of rain water stands proudly by the main gate.

It's not uncommon for thirsty passers-by to take a drink from it, knowing that it will be clean and fresh. Perfect, massive headed flowers hang in breathtaking splendour from baskets all along the front of Barley's wide fronted barn.

Barley's farm is a farm of flower meadows, thick stout oak trees and corn flowers. Plump brown hens pick at the rich grass verges at the side of the road. Red hens search further down the lane. These are real ginger hens, plump, clean and bright with glowing feathers. They lay gorgeous, big, brown eggs.

They are not a bit like the scrawny, undernourished, frail creatures with bald patches and clumps of feathers missing, that you see in South American countries, scratching in vain in the hot dust with diseases and sores.

Barley's place is a model farm. There is field after field of rich barley. Fields of barely are different in these times. The barley stalks are much longer and thicker than the modified barley of more recent times. As such this barley is more prone to being "laid"; pushed over in great swathes by the wind and the rain that comes this way.

The corn fields are also full of bright, wild flowers because there are no pesticides and even if there were, the farmers would never have the money to pay for them. As a result, productivity is low and every inch of land and far greater effort is needed to produce the required amount of grain to feed all the mouths in the country. The fields are kept small and hedges around them are kept high in an attempt to provide shelter from the weather. There are more dykes, better drainage but better diversity.

The people and the flora and fauna live side by side on the land in a kind of natural balance, the way it has been for hundreds of years, the way it was always meant to be.

Despite approaching his fortieth year, Barley still hasn't quite grown up yet. He still isn't married, even though he's been courting for years. They say it's because his dad died young and as the only son he took over the farm before he was 'left school', before he was really grown up. He became a 'half grown', labouring hard on the farm to get all the chores done but also fitting in time to play. And this became his routine, a routine which he's stuck with. He has never been beyond climbing the tallest tree, to look into a new nest, or spending time fluffing up a favourite chicken, like it was going to be entered in a show. Some blame his mother. She is old and wizened but still as tough as a metal trap.

The day is still very young. It's bright but still shimmers with the night cold. Old Mrs Green stands in the open door of the farm house. An old man is walking past on the way to buy an early morning paper.

Mrs Green wants to know if it's icy.

Mrs Green:

"Slayarp?" she shouts.

The old man shrugs.

Old Man:

"Aayhs think."

Mrs Green implores Barley to take his pullover with him, on his way back out to the fields with his livestock.

Mrs Green:

"Barley! You'd better grab your ganzy."

Most farmers of this time, play some part in the management and custody of nature. They see it as part of their role. This part of the job isn't about profit, it's about doing what's expected, it's about doing what's right. But Barley takes this to another level. His farm is a sort of unofficial animal sanctuary. Any rescued animal; injured, found, abandoned, can always find a

home on Barley's farm. He is the local hero when it comes to animal rescue. This ensures there is always a steady stream of injured pigeons and owls with broken wings, turning up on his door step. Some of the children dream up more grandiose schemes and they know they'll always get a fair hearing from Barley, even if no one else is interested. He's seen it all. "Grecian 2000 for Greyhounds" and "More Homes for Homing Pigeons" to name just the most recent.

There is work to be done on every farm but there is more work to be done on this farm than anywhere else. All the usual tasks have to be completed - collecting eggs and baskets of apples, smoking, moaning about the weather, sleeping in the orchard amongst the blossom. But who else cleans out owls nests? The grandest castles are made out of straw bales on Barley's farm. Straw bales are so versatile – to build tunnels, dens, houses, towers. Memories of golden corn linger forever – souvenirs of Summer and barns full of gold into the bargain in which to kiss the very sweetest girls.

Further along from Barley's we come to Hubert Harrison's small holding. Hubert, like many of the locals, is a market gardener. He grows crops intensely on his few rich acres and sells them on a stall in the market in Toffee Town each Saturday. It's hard work but provides quite a good living from a modest piece of land. Hubert is in his kitchen deciding what to have for his breakfast. Market gardeners start early but one of the perks is that they get to start work after light, unlike the farmers who have their animals to look after. They still all have gravy running through their veins.

Hubert:

"I don't know whether to have porridge for breakfast which is boring, or whether I should have toast which'll kill me."

Hubert's Wife:

"Well we don't have much bread."

Hubert:

"I'll have toast then. No I won't, I'll have porridge. I'll live a bit longer and become even more grumpy."

Moving on from Hubert's place, we pass Snortey's apple and goose farm, where he mainly grows raspberries and soon we come to the village proper.

2. Mabel's General Store

Swinging sharp left we arrive at the very heart of the village. Straight away we come to Mabel's General store. Welcome to heaven. It's a tiny place but it's absolutely packed to the rafters with goodies, sweets, toffees, chocolates, liquorice, cigarettes, tobacco, toys. The place is so packed that you can't even get inside. There's only ever room for Mabel and despite being a tiny old lady, even she struggles to squeeze in between the stacks of boxes. She basically sells everything that "won't go off." And anything she hasn't got, which is rare, "It'll be in next Tuesday."

The cash register is definitely pounds shillings and pence. Decimalisation was not a concept that ever really took hold in this shop.

Mabel:
"That'll be five shillings and sixpence please. Oh hold on a minute, I'll convert it to decimal."

At that point you know you are in for a long wait.

Then after about five minutes of head shaking and a great deal of sucking on a small black pencil and scribbling she'll concede, "It's still five shillings and six pence."

The other great thing about Mabel is that she's always open, twenty four hours a day, seven days a week – longer when necessary. Knock on her door any time, day or night, hail or shine and she'll serve you. She'll moan every time but she'll always serve you.

Mabel:

"You must want your hear'd testin' cumin' 'art on a neet lark this.

Anybody who comes owt tanart must be..."

You're never too early and never too late. If ever she's not in the shop (or standing immediately outside it if she's just had a delivery) you just knock on her cottage door across the way.

There is nothing fresh in Mabel's store, no cheese, no vegetables, no fruit. This provides a great source of mischief and fun for local youths. A constant stream of children, from far and wide, delight in getting Mabel out in the rain to ask for a pound of apples or a quarter of cheese – just for the mischief of it.

Boys take it in turn to knock her up and ask for...

Boy1:

"A pound of lemons please!"

Boy2:

"Me mother sent me for four lamb chops."

Saving up to get paper money, (not an easy task in these times) so that you can shop at Mabel's and see her struggle to find the change, is another local pass-time amongst the younger generation. It encourages the boys of the village to save as much of their pocket money as possible.

The ultimate aim is to save and save until you get five pounds which you duly change into a five pound note. Boys will do anything to reach this goal, walking dogs for a penny a time, sweeping huge stack yards for a shilling. After months of labouring and scrimping and having reached Nirvana, they hurriedly cycle round to Mabel's and buy ....

Boy1:

"A penny bubbly!"

... for which they duly hand over their hard won five pound note.

Mabel:

"Haven't yu got now't smaller?"

Boy1:

"No – it's the smallest I've got."

Mabel always struggles to come up with the change but she never turns the business away.

Boy1:

"I want one of them boxes of chocolates."

The boy points to a box of chocolates with 'Happy Mother's Day' written on the side. They are under a large pile of other boxes of chocolates which Mabel struggles to move out of the way.

Mabel:

"Do you want them wrapped?"

Boy1:

"No I'll eat them now."

It all adds to the magic. And what magic there is. Sweets of every conceivable flavour, shape and colour, are stacked enticingly in huge glass jars on every inch of shelf space. Adventurers had to fight with evil serpents in far off jungle lands to find such spices. They probably had to kill too. Liquorice, aniseed, gum Arabic, sherbet dip, toffee crisp, Turkish delight. Caramac and cigarettes in packs of five are handed over in fistfuls. Flavours too numerous to mention and here they all are for sale in Mrs Mabel Goodwood's

shop window, all the wonders of the world and most for a penny a chew. Treats from far flung places, distant, unknown, maybe not even marked on any proper map, unknown places where few civilised people have ever ventured, like Africa, Spain and even Wales.

3. The Chippy

Moving along the street, further into the village, we pass a few more pretty farms and a variety of dainty cottages before shortly arriving at "the Chippy". Here fish is steeped for days in milk before being deep fried in the finest beef lard, over a coal stoked griddle. Truly there is no finer flavour of food anywhere in the land, yet it's reckoned you have to be born in the village to really appreciate the true depth of flavour.

People across the village watch out for the smoke appearing out of the chip shop chimney, just like people in Rome watch for signs of smoke at the Vatican when a new Pope is being elected. Huge queues form outside the Chippy, often stretching back to the Coop and beyond. People wait with inordinate patience for the time when the white fleshed chips are declared, "ready".

"One of each and some bits," gets you a fish in crisp batter, a portion of soft roasted chips and a portion of the flakes of fine crumbly batter that fall from the fish and are given away in generous portions.

Fish is seen by many as pauper food at this time. Middle aged men turn their noses up at the thought of a fish supper. They love the taste but they are conscious of the stigma.

Father1:

"No one saw you buy this fish did they?"

But no man alive could pass the Chippy without calling in to get a paper of chips.

4. The Joiners' Arms.

A few steps on from the chip shop and we come to what many in the village consider to be their spiritual home, the village pub. Every manner of human activity is carried out within these four walls of the Joiners' Arms. All business is transacted. Livestock, cattle, sheep, horses and houses are bought and sold. Marriages are proposed, fights are started and both won and lost. Bachelors look for wives and wives look for husbands. People settle differences and start new ones. Weddings, anniversaries and funerals are marked or celebrated or ignored, all within these walls.

Even the dead drink here, long after the other customers have left. Often this is not until very late into the night.

This pub sells quite a range of brews. There's the blackest beer, thick like treacle tar. Other brews glow radiant, clear, bright, orange with endless fizzing bubbles.

Broken teeth are scattered across the car park. Some local children genuinely believe the tooth fairy deposits them here. For now the pub is quiet for it is still early morn. There's no one at the bar, save for a single lone drinker. The ghosts still have it and they drink quiet and respectfully and mostly invisibly. Their rowdy days are behind them.

The lone drinker is an interloper, a stranger passing through, himself not much more than a ghost. He stands at the bar sipping a large glass of ice cold brandy. He asked Sleepy Dawson the way. Sleepy gave garbled instructions then said,

Sleepy Dawson:

"And I don't tell lies. Never told a lie. Don't even know how. I must 'ave bin away when they taught it at school."

Everyone in the village knows Sleepy tells nowt but lies. No wonder the stranger is drinking so hard, so early in the morning. He must be wondering if this is the village that never sleeps, or the village that never wakes up.

For now we'll seek out the life of the stirring village but later we'll return to the Joiners' when those with living thirsts have found their way back through the doors.

Whistle Wood

5. Wilf the Coalman

Next to the Joiners' comes Wilf the Coalman. Wilf's yard is piled high with a mountain of coal but getting any delivered has always been a terrible challenge. You see Wilf is about eighty years old and only about four feet tall. He weighs significantly less than any of his sacks of coal, even though he only half fills them these days. They talk about weigh-lifters lifting more than their own weight, well Wilf has to do this about two hundred times a day and has done every working day for the last sixty years, just to load his wagon. Then he has to drive it all round the village and drag it all off the lorry again, bag by bag and heave it up people's steps and into their coal house or cellar. Little surprise he finds delivering "the coil" a challenge. People are always pushing increasingly desperate notes through his door...

"Send ten bags, TODAY!!! PLEASE!!!"

You might get two bags if you're lucky. Strangely though, no one ever runs out of coal. You see Wilf knows exactly what everybody has in their cellars and he knows how fast they burn it. Single-handedly he keeps the village supplied.

Immediately outside Wilf's yard, stands the main village bus stop. An old Italian refugee, a displaced person from the war, stands patiently with a box of homemade ice cream. The old guy travels the buses all day for free, selling his ice cream to the other passengers as he travels. It's a secret recipe. Very popular with all the locals, as is the man who makes it, although no one can really pronounce his name. Many are afraid he'll die suddenly and the recipe will be lost forever. As if by magic it never melts until you buy one. It conjures up the taste of sea air, sea breeze, a place with plenty of donkeys but no rock.

The Isle isn't far from the coast, across the plains of North Lincolnshire but the sea is too far to see, despite the frequent strains of children at the highest point of the hill.

Older children, some in their late teens, also stand waiting at the bus stop. They are going off to the Grammar school in Toffee Town to pursue their learning. Not everyone in the village is convinced by the merits of education nor supportive of those seeking to better themselves.

Curly:

"Tha can cut a coo in haffe on payaper tha' knaws?"

A middle aged man is standing waiting for the bus beside the students. Curly Johnston would normally be on his way to the fields. He works piece work which means he gets paid for what he achieves. He starts earlier and works longer and harder than any other man in the village. He can pull an acre of sugar beet in a week at the start of the season in October for which he gets paid £30. It's horse work but normal wages are just thirty shillings per day so he makes at least three times more than any man on daily rates. It takes a lot for Curly to miss work but today he has no choice.

He has the most severe toothache and for that there is only one solution. He's on his way to a nearby village to Butcher Bryant's dental surgery. Butcher Bryant is indeed a butcher as well as the local dentist. You see there isn't enough money in teeth at this time – it's just a means to boost the income from the butchers shop. Besides, whilst they are round having their teeth drawn, they might just purchase a few rashers of bacon or a pound of best mince and onion.

Butcher Bryant cuts a terrifying sight. He's a fiery, red haired Scot with red cheeks and blooded apron. You have to be in desperate need to go round there, in desperate need of an extraction because that's all he does on the dentistry side. And he's none too subtle about it either.

Dental Patient:

"Will it hurt?"

Butcher Bryant:

"Aye of course it will but you have to cause pain to cure pain don't you?"

Cheering words indeed.

6. Pretty Farms And The Village Cafe

Further along the street we pass more pretty farms. The buildings are distinctly Georgian, with their distinctive thin, gravy coloured brick and large, solid looking windows. There are stack yards next to each farm house, home to huge, round stacks of bountiful straw and hay. The stacks are properly thatched with sloping roofs and each has a corn dolly perched proudly at the crest. This is an ancient tradition and in these times traditions are guarded jealously. It's like the generations can feel change coming so they go out of their way to hold on to what they can, whilst ever they are able.

Pearling wanders off to collect his cows. He's several hours late. They'll be braying. In fact he's nearly always several hours late, so much so that it's become their routine. The cows would miss it if he ever turned up early like he's supposed to.

Some middle aged women are already sweating at their toil on the farms. They are sexing chickens.

They basically act as judge and jury. Life is in their very hands. Day old chicks are moved from a tray and are put down either to the right or the left. Life can be gone in a second. The female chicks are kept for laying. The males go for fattening for the table. Some types of chicken don't make good layers and others are not good for the table, so depending on the gender and type of a chicken, life can be very short lived. Even in these times, farms have to pay their way and there is no room for sentimentality.

Whistle Wood is unusual in boasting a cafe but the service this provides is very much needed here. This is an area where many people have signed 'the Pledge'. They strictly avoid alcohol, except for medicinal purposes of course. When there's a cattle market or fair, some people choose to meet in the cafe, rather than the pub, especially if they are hoping to do business with the abstainers. The cafe is owned and run by Mervin Mendall. Mervin is reputed to be the great grand nephew of an infamous Nazi poisoner. His intention is to run a quiet eatery in an out of the way place, which just happens to be here.

An inspector with clipboard stands in Wellington boots in Mervin's cafeteria. He wears bicycle clips around his trouser bottoms in a vain attempt to stop the rats climbing up his trouser legs. He marks down on his clipboard every time he sees a rat. There are a lot of marks on his paper. In fact his biro pen has almost run dry with all the marking.

Mervin:

"I think you've already counted that one," argues Mervin as he swats hopelessly at a rat with a tea towel. It isn't the best advert for trade.

It's ironic really. Mervin has no time for pets normally.

Mervin:

"The only place for animals in the home is on the plate."

But there's plenty of room for animals in this cafe.

7. The Post Office

Moving along now from the cafe, past a few more village centre houses, we come to the village post office at the foot of Candy Hill. This is the home and work place of post master Mr Angus William Andrew Kenneth Bruce-McDonald, known to everyone in the village and everyone who knows him from far and wide simply as 'Jock'.

Jock is tall, fat and bald, save for two small tufts of jet black brylcreemed hair, one on each side of his big fat head. He looks like Buddha in big thick glasses. He sweats endlessly and has several large butter dripping chins. For all the world he looks Italian, with his dark skin, permanent bruised looking eyes, his big stomach and thick dark glasses. Whatever else could mark a man out to be more Italian? But he isn't Italian at all, he's from deepest, darkest Glasgow.

There's a hand written sign in Jock's shop window, written in biro, in shaky handwriting, "Remember to address letters properly!"

The irony is lost on no one. Of all the people in the village, there isn't enough room on a standard envelope to write Jock's name on it in full. Jock is the self appointed enforcer and arbitrator of "the rule of law."

Jock:

"You haven't been putting out washing on a Sunday again have you Missus?

You'll be getting a summons."

He'd like to see the people who let their horses walk on the grass verge across from the post office get a summons but the local bobby isn't interested.

It's an unusual post office. Jock has everything you'd expect on his shelves; stamps, writing paper, pens, birthday cards, balls of string, dust ...etc. He also sells hardware, drinking glasses, seeds, boots, and watering cans and he offers a good selection of sandwiches. Sandwiches from a post office? Well you lick stamps don't you?

Jock is infamous for his customer service and serving etiquette.

Customer:

"A sandwich please Mr Post Master."

Jock:

"Chaase or meeat?"

Customer:

"What kind of meat is it?"

Jock:

"Do you want a f*cking sandwich or don't you?"

The local magistrates know Jock well and impose further punishment on miscreants who come before them by insisting that summonses are paid by postal order – sufficient additional punishment to straighten out some of the otherwise most disreputable characters.

You can tell by the colour of his face that Jock's blood pressure is sky high – it's always that way. There are so many irritations for him in this job – so many petty rules and regulations which he can't help but adhere to. He spends his day handing out the Governments money to the old, the sick and the dying and he resents every single penny of it. With trembling hands his nightmare never ends and he can not resist checking that they have all complied with the rules.

Jock:

"Have you bought a license for that dog?"

Jock:

"You ought to get your rates paid."

Jock:

"Have you got a license for that pony?"

Customer:

"A license for a pony?"

P.J. Naughton

Jock:

"Well think on!"

Jock spends much of his time cursing his customers. He loves horse racing and he has it on his television in the post office, whenever it's being broadcast, which is every weekday afternoon starting from about midday.

Jock:

"You would come in just as this horse race is about to start wouldn't you?"

Jock's wife - Big Mau (pronounced Mow, proper name Maureen, bad limp, varicose veins) is the post lady. In sharp contrast to Jock she is laid back, back slapping and jolly, all the more amazing after being married to Jock for so many long years. She was induced which may or may not account for her prolific bad language which she struggles to control.

Big Mau:

"A second delivery? On a Sunday? They can fu, fu, fu, forget that."

Jock has a pathological hatred of cats. So it was most unfortunate for a stray cat to sneak upstairs into his bedroom on the very day he got a new bed. Certainly the cat's luck was out that day because it was Jock who found it asleep on his brand new bed.

Jock:

"Of all the bloody houses in't village and it had to pick mine!"

The local police sergeant declared the bedroom a crime scene but the cat was never found. The police couldn't reach any conclusions. Some say it must have run up the chimney and had a heart attack and died. Others say it must have squeezed under the closed door. No evidence was ever found. The case remains unsolved unto this very day.

8. Candy Hill

Where ever you turn from the post office, you're going to go up hill from here, unless you turn back on yourself and go back the way you've come. We could go straight ahead up Tower Hill but we are going to turn left up Candy Hill instead, up this steep, staircase lane.

This takes us on to the local council estate. These houses are all rented from the local authority. They are strong houses, well maintained with large, neat gardens and clean, bright, gleaming, highly polished, door steps. Door steps are cleaned at least once every day on this estate. The shame of an unclean door step would be too much to bear even for the most modest household. Clackadahlias and Gladioliacs stand straight and bright in nearly every garden. The lane is narrow but crowded with people busy and hurrying. There are no cars. In fact there are less than half a dozen cars in the entire village at this time and none of them are owned by people on this hill. People are milling about, getting on with the start of their day.

Despite the hurry, nearly everyone has time to stop and catch up on the latest gossip. Some are talking only to themselves and even then, some of them are arguing.

Inquests are well underway as to the happenings of the previous night. Undiscovered animals inhabit this area. They're undiscovered largely because no one has ever bothered to look for them. There are animals that only ever come out during the night, who live only during the drinking hours so they are never believed, even when they are seen. A husband and wife are sitting at the breakfast table...

Wife:

"So you saw a lobster walking down the High Street in Church Town last night did you?"

Husband:

"Honest dear I did."

Wife:

"And I suppose it was carrying a handbag?"

Husband:

"It was dear, it was – did you see it as well?"

Wife:

"The shame of it! And I suppose you hadn't been to see Madam Lulu down at the Joiners' Arms by any chance?"

Husband:

"On my word dear, on my very word."

Old Walt & Daisy live at the foot of the hill. Walt's bad and arsy again. He has spent his life cutting the dykes with a scythe for Trent Catchment. He'd normally be on the banks by this time but he's got a bad back and he's off sick, so he's sitting on a hard wooden kitchen chair, just outside his front door with his wife.

Young Mother1:
(passing by pushing a pram...)
"Good Morning Mr Mowner. How are you?"

Whistle Wood

Old Walt:

"It's me back. It's goin' to rain."

Daisy:

"It's too cold."

Old Walt:

"There's always some' at. "

Daisy:

"It's too dry an' all."

Old Walt:

"And when it 'int too cold it's too hot be haffe!"

Daisy:

"It's too nothing if you ask me.

Old Walt:

"And too everything!"

The young mother nods with a knowing smile and walks on by. Walt's lived a hard life, cutting and slashing endlessly at the undergrowth along the banks of the rivers, waging war, endless war on the brambles and nettles and tall reeds, putting everything in to win each battle, only to know that the same battles would have to be fought again, in the very same place, next year.

It's a hard meagre living, scything the river banks and ditches, sinking in the warp, the glue like mud, retrieving lost Wellington boots and sunken oil drums, watching out for lightening strikes, for it is well known that thunder follows the rivers; contending with the unrelenting, endless Summer heat that buzzes with flies and loneliness; silence echoing across the Lincolnshire Tundra, competing in pointless moans and complaints and enduring the endless raw chaffing, sprains and pains and pulled muscles, just to keep the drain channels open along with hundreds just exactly like him.

These old men live like war time rationing is still on, for to them the memory of the war is still very fresh. Many of them were sent away to fight and they are waiting and watching for the next war to come along. They suspect they won't have long to wait.

These old men still dig for victory. Only a small part of their large gardens is given over to a small patch of lawn and flowers. The vast majority of "their" land is used to raise base vegetables - potatoes, cabbage, leeks, onions and parsnips are grown with real purpose. It's about survival. Pies are used to store potatoes just like on the farms proper – large piles of potatoes are covered in straw and soil to protect them from the frost so that they will last throughout the Winter.

Old Walt:

(talking aloud to himself...)

"The land is too low round here. It's too dry.

"This land's no good. You can't grow 'owt. Just weeds. And do the council do 'owt aboot it?"

Daisy:

"Bugger all."

Walt:

"That's it. Bugger all.

And are they bothered?"

Daisy:

"You're not wrong Walt. You're not wrong."

Old Walt: (talking to himself...)

"Place an't bin the same since they put sewage in. And Tally wag pooh-alls – they're always meddling. No it an't bin the sem' and it probably never will be neither if you ask me."

Children run up the street shouting with excitement. They are ready for school but are ragged and you can still see the stains of yesterday around their mouths and they are running up the hill, the wrong way. Something serious has to be happening.

Children:

"The rent man's coming!"

Something serious indeed! The wives don't know whether to believe them but several scurry off to hide – just in case. Others continue the morning's deliberations. Everything has an order in these times. Order provides certainty and as a community, a lot of effort is put in to guarding and protecting the rhythm of their lives, it provides something of a sense of security. Washing is done each and every Monday. "Toad in the Hole" is served on Tuesdays. Brass is polished on Wednesdays. Leave it until a Thursday and you risk being vilified.

Two young mothers are chatting...

Young Mother 1:
"He can't work he's on tablets you know!"

Young Mother 2:
"Do they let them have tablets in prison?"

Young Mother 1:
"Do you know, you'll never guess, she put her washing out on a Sunday."

Young Mother 2:

"I bet she boiled those nappies an' all."

A wolf howls over on the Trossocks somewhere.

Young Mother 1:

"She's expecting again you know?"

Young Mother 2:

"What and with her Reggie away?"

Young Mother 1:

"I wonder who's responsible this time?"

Young Mother 2:

"Doesn't the last one look like the postman?"

Young Mother 1:

"Well he can't work you know, he's on tablets."

The two young mothers part in fits of giggles.

In a matter of seconds, Councillor Fry comes walking briskly up the street. He doubles as the rent man. The children were correct. Years of experience have taught him to pounce at speed, hoping to catch his poor unfortunate prey unawares. He moves with speed and as much stealth as he can muster. Like a lion with the smell of blood in its nostrils, he sniffs the air, before deciding to veer along the left hand side of the street.

Rent Man:

"Rent!"

And without knocking he opens a door and walks straight into Lucy Lockett's debt laden abode. These are serious times. Miss two weeks rent and you'll be evicted and your possessions auctioned off to clear your debt - known locally as "being sold up." It is an all too frequent occurrence for many of the local residents.

Mr Hardy, the meths drinker, known as "Smart", stands smartly, across the road with his head propped up against the wall of old Sam's yard.

Smart has scorched his insides, he's burnt with drink. He lives in the village – well at least in the gutters and the provinces, for he has never had a proper home. He always chuckles to himself when he sees the rent-man collecting, for he knows that without a home he is immune from the attentions of the debt collector. He served in the Warwickshire Guards for twenty five years but was demobbed at the end of the war, having grown too old to be of any use to the armed services. He's never known any other job but continues his soldiering as best he can, at least the best he can with so much drink inside him. He has almost drunk himself to malt, the Genie sprite from the bottle.

For a homeless man he certainly takes his responsibilities seriously. He stands guard over the village each and every day and night and continues his routines much as he has always done. He rigorously cleans his kit each day, without fail. His boots are highly polished every morning and he scrubs the white enamel mug with the chipped blue rim that he was given when he was demobbed but he's had no inspection for nigh on twenty years. He spends his days marching and standing to. It's what he knows. He dreams of leave but he never gets any. His only responsibility in the world apart from himself and the protection of the village is to a large, long haired, scruffy, black mongrel dog called "Blackie." Blackie is a Heinz dog, fifty seven different varieties. The dog is groomed, disciplined, inspected, fed, trained, marched, tied up, bedded down, rested. It's a strict regime.

Years ago, Smart once had 'LOVE' and 'HATE' tattooed across his knuckles, 'LOVE' across his right hand and 'HATE' across his left but since an unfortunate accident towards the end of his military career when he lost the little finger on his left hand, he has since been left with...

"LOVE – HAT."

Someone once asked why he didn't just have 'CONDOM' tattooed across his forehead. This wasn't a wise thing to ask a man who specialised in boxing in the army.

Mostly though, Smart is a quiet man who is slow to anger. He sleeps mostly above the furnace in the brick yard at the edge of the village, above the glowing embers. He rarely strays far from the precincts of the factory and the brick toilet block, except to venture into town each day to carry out his patrols and guard duty. He is drawn by the permanence of the place and all those bricks.

Sometimes Smart's friend 'Blister' calls by to stay. He's as drunk as Smart but much more unkempt. No one really knows where he comes from but people surmise he's from the sea side some where because he tends to arrive more frequently in Winter, drawn to the warmth of Smart's gaff. Some say he's got a daughter somewhere but no one really knows.

Child:

"Where did Blister come from Mam?"

Mother:

"Eeeh I dunna know."

Father:

"He arrived long ago."

Mother:

"He came from a place which no one really knows."

Mrs Beaver, rent unpaid, is next up the hill.

Gossip1:

"She's had the grocer knocking again!"

Gossip2:

"And the electric man."

Gossip3:

"The gas man would have been knocking as well if she'd got gas."

Gossip1:

"The coalman went away with a smile."

Gossip3:

"Imagine the state of her sheets."

Mrs Beaver's dog skips by on its endless Odyssey. It's an incredible dog although to look at it, it's nothing remarkable, just a small, black, shorthaired mongrel - very ordinary. It spends its life roaming the village, circling endlessly at will. This dog walks so far it often skips by on three legs, as it suffers from blisters on its badly worn feet. It's always on the move and travels freely about the village all day long. At night when the pub turns out, Mrs Beaver pops a lead on the dog and takes it out for a walk. No dog was ever less in need of a walk but dog walking makes a great excuse for observing, at first hand, the drunken scandals, the illicit liaisons, the drunken fights, the swearing and abuse.

Mrs Beaver's son 'Elvis' is nearly seventeen. He works tirelessly on the construction of his very own motorcycle. It's a Frankenstein machine, built out of many different motor cycles of different makes and models.

Elvis has been struggling to get all the parts to fit together for years and has only recently found that a piece from his mother's table lamp is just the piece he needed to get the bike to finally fit together. It's a "650cc Norton Commander, Ariel 4, Super Cruise, Bonneville, Triumph Hellcat, Honda, Yamaha, Thunderbolt, BSA, Motto Guzzi, Light Shade". If only he could get it started!

Elvis's best friend 'Casanova', best friends ever since they started school together, is a real hit with the girls. He knows it's impossible to please all the people, all the time but he certainly has had a good go at pleasing a good half of them.

Mr Beaver, father of Elvis, is the village paid rat catcher. He struggles through most nights with a struggling bag of struggling. Sometimes he's catching – sometimes he's releasing. He secretly breeds his quarry in his coalhouse. He finds it's better for business that way.

Next door to the Beavers, lives John Joseph, retired miner who lives for beer and poetry. Mr Joseph cooks chips, large thin slices of potato, cooked brown in boiled beef fat on their open fire. The chips are served with lashings of tomato sauce. Delicious. He's frying bacon rind too on the fire. It's hissing and spitting – causing an occasional flash of flames. He's a genuine scholar, who once, long ago, strutted the land, a prince of learning, golden and glowing. At some point in the distant past, in the buzz of the town, he zeroed his woman and had to give it all up and spent his working life driving a shovel instead, to earn an honest crust.

He has no money but Mr Joseph is the richest man alive. He has standards and values. He lives in a 'make believe' world. He's long since given up on reality. He lives in a world of powdery flowers where the sun always shines but never burns anyone, a world of poetry and love, a world full of jokes and smiles, a world without pain or retribution, a world without anger or regret. After all, these things only exist because we let them. Some say the change was gradual. I guess the going was just too steep for him, out in the real world. He just made his own world and moved into that and is happy living there.

He spends his life trying to write the words those lying in the graveyard would have said, had they had one more breath left in their body – had they been able to speak just a few more words. He also tries to write the words they would want to say now. He doesn't work. His wife struggles. The garden is left to grow wild, save for the path walked by Mrs Joseph to the washing line each and every morning.

Mr Joseph has lost all contact with his hard days down the mines but Mrs Joseph hasn't. She still consumes fifteen boxes of "Top Mill" snuff, well wrapped in an anonymous brown paper bag every week. No one is supposed to know but everybody does. It's one of the few links left between the area and the founding fathers of Virginia. How strange. I bet they never thought anything like that would happen before they set off for their New World.

Immediately opposite the Joseph's lives Roaring-Meg. Roaring-Meg roars at little LittleBoyo, her son. As usual she is bellowing and roaring. Children spattle except the youngest.

Little Percy picks up the yard brush and pushes it straight through one of the remaining glass panes in the front door. He then proceeds to climb through the new gap.

Roaring Meg:

"You little bastard, I'll cut your throat."

But she doesn't. Months later, there'll still be wet cardboard in that window. Love seeps through the fabric of the village like water seeping through a limestone cave. It's incredible but somehow the water cuts through the stone and so it is with the sentiment in this community.

As always the women on the street ignore this fresh disturbance. They have more important things to discuss. There has been a death over night.

The Death Of Mrs Chester Jones

Woman 1:

"Have you heard?
Mrs Chester Jones has died."

Woman 2:

"Candle Harris's sister?"

Woman 1:

"That's right. Brenda."

Woman 2:

"Never! How can she have died?
She can't have been more than fifty seven."

Woman 1:

"Oh yes. I knew it was coming like.
We were related you know – her niece was my husband's brother's sister in law. We never spock."

(There's a common game played by villagers and that is to pick two local people at random and to work out how they are related. It's always possible to find a link, everyone is related to everyone else at least in some way - cousins, third cousins once removed, Uncle's in-laws' Auntie, their cat ran up our passage.)

Woman 2:

"Well I'll never. I wonder who'll cop for that lot?"

Woman 1: (whispering...)

"It'll be Chelmsford - Chester's half brother I reckon."

Woman 2:

"Is he still going?"

Woman 1:

"Turned ninety six a week last Wednesday and he's still chasing Alice."

Woman 2: (laughing...)
"He'll have given up on Brenda now then."

Woman 1: (whispering quieter...)
"She had – you know. They say her husband brought it back from the trenches but I'm not so sure."

Woman 2:
"Well they didn't have women in the trenches did they?"

Woman 1:
"Funeral's on Thursday.
Internment at one.
Reception in the Joiners'. Sandwiches at two."

Woman 2:
"I bet it'll be meat paste."

Woman 1:
"Probably knowing them."

Woman 2:

"And with all their money."

Woman 1:

"That's why they have it."

Woman 2:

"Aye. They never spend any."

Sally Slack-Cabbage is struggling as ever to get her brother Norman off to work. He's suffering badly from the bucket load of Guinness he drank the night before.

Sally:

"It's time to wake up."

Norman:

"It's too early."

Sally:

"No it's your time to get up, you'll be late for work."

Norman:

"It's too dark."

Sally:

"It's not dark at all. Besides no matter how light it is, it's still your time to get up."

Norman:

"I got up yesterday."

Sally:

"Yes and you have to get up forever more."

Norman rolls over in his sheet and curses the light. Sally has been thumbing through the Sunday supplement. She's particularly interested in the article, 'Our fifty top tips to improve your orgasm.' The trouble is she can't understand forty seven of them and she can't get the other three to work.

Mrs Prissy Coleman

George Dabb, known by one and all as the paraffin man, (mainly because he spends his life delivering paraffin,) drives the local hardware van; keen prices, huge range of stock. In these times hardware means buckets of nails, wire netting and paraffin. He meets Mrs Coleman as she steps from her front door into the street, preened, powdered and tidy like a small wasp but her smalls flap like semaphore flags on the washing line in her yard.

As always she is accompanied by her well groomed Scottie dog. 'Toots' sports a bright red ribbon and a small silver bell. He's her only mark of respectability other than her appearance. Her gooses' nest preening boudoir certainly brings her no credit from those who have seen it or from the rest of the village inhabitants who have heard about it. She rarely opens the curtains but people have seen the mess her house is in.

Her husband is in prison – he must have done something really bad because he's in long term but she pretends he's dead. She tells people she goes to see relatives down in London on the train but it seems strange that she always goes with penal regularity on the last Monday in every month. It all sounds a bit too much.

The Paraffin Man:

"Hello Mrs Coleman how's your husband?"

Mrs Coleman:

"He's dead."

The Paraffin Man:

"I'm very sorry to hear that. Remember me to him when you see him. I hope he gets better soon."

She sets off in a huff, along the cobbled street, walking with her characteristic fast, short, clipped steps. She clicks her bright polished heeled shoes rhythmically and clutches tight on to her small, black, leather handbag. She's in a hurry. She has a train to catch and does her best to ignore the other women in the street.

The sun is building high above the village now. The streets are warming as baking is drawn from ovens. Women miether competitively. Most of the children are now in school, at least those who are going. Some children don't attend. Some absent themselves with their parents consent, mostly to help out on the land. Some abscond without their parents' knowledge. Others attend in the morning, then abscond later on during the day.

Empty toffee jars are traded about the town like currency, they are like gold to the old women who use them to pickle onions in and just about anything else. Gallon upon gallon of vinegar is hauled up hill and dale and into just about every kitchen and scullery in the village. Onions, walnuts, eggs, shallots, beetroot, fruit – anything that can be preserved is soaked, boiled, washed, peeled and finally immersed for months in acrid vinegar, usually accompanied by cloves and peppercorn spices.

As cash tills ring about the village and purses begin to empty, more and more tradesmen are turned away out of necessity.

Mrs Beaver:

"Not today thank you!"

No wonder the tradesmen like to get round early.

Kindly Mr and Mrs Humbug, always with a smile, and a kindly word and a small paper bag of sweets, both striped and boiled, happen along the street. They are wearing the smart rain coats that they always wear, even though they are far too hot for a day like this but it's the only decent clothes they have. Mr Humbug lifts his trilby and smiles politely to everyone that he meets on the street.

Old Squirrel is being brought back by ambulance from hospital after his third heart attack.

Old Squirrel:

"Just drop me off at the pub."

Ambulance Driver:

"I'm sorry Mr Jackson, we can't. We have to see you home. It's more than our jobs are worth."

And after dropping Squirrel off, before they've turned the ambulance round, he is on his way back down the hill towards the pub, puffing like a train on his pipe as he skis without skis, on two sticks down to his favourite watering hole, the only place he wants to go.

At the top of the hill, Mr Cuckoo Walters is digging in his garden. It's a show piece garden, full of row after neat row of wonderfully adolescent, luscious vegetables. He's one of the old men still digging for victory but he's not sure who against. A homemade sign standing at the edge of the garden which overlooks the street announces– 'Honey for sale'. He only sells about six jars a year but when anyone knocks on his door with the intention of buying a jar, he always moans.

Mr Walters:

"Not another one!"

Old Flora, his wife, known to most as Flo, is a few years older than Cuckoo. She's grown very feeble both in mind and body. She waves her heavy, mahogany umbrella angrily at anyone passing in the street. Almost everyone ignores her but those who know her best just wish her well.

The Walters have lived in virtually every house in the village. Flora has suffered every illness, every disease she has ever heard of. She sits in the doctor's waiting room each morning eating her breakfast. Along with all the others she waits her turn to be told.

Doctor:

"You don't smoke and you're not over weight so it's got to be your age."

She usually has a bucket of sick with her, proof of the night's suffering. Mrs Walters is on tablets of course. Lots of tablets. She takes every opportunity to explain this to anyone who she thinks might be remotely interested.

P.J. Naughton

Elderly Gent:

(on entering Doctor's surgery...)

"Hello Mrs Walters. And how are you?"

Mrs Walters:

"I'm on twenty seven tablets and I'm still badly. These doctors you just can't trust them. They haven't got a clue what's wrong with me. No idea at all. "

She is the bane of Councillor Fry's life.

Mrs Walters:

"Councillor you're just going to have to move me."

He must have heard that at least five hundred times.

Mrs Walters:

"It's no good, I can't manage up on that hill."

A few months later...

Mrs Walters:

"I need to be back up on the hill."

On one occasion he took them around the village in his car and asked them to point at any house they wanted, he was so distraught, so desperate to get them settled. It still didn't work though. They've had six houses since and all them in less than twelve months.

At the present time they are living at the top or at least as near to the top as Mr Fry could last achieve. A few more steps and eventually we reach the very crest of the hill.

9. View From The Top

That hill leaves most people, young and old alike, with uneven breath but it's a price worth paying. The view is truly fantastic. The full vista of the unspoilt countryside opens up in a splendid pallet of colour.

The miracle of what man has achieved, simply by digging the soil to the depth of a plough share, some times only to the depth of a spade, stretches out before us. This land is a fantastic portrait painted from the artist's pallet of strawberries and bright green beans and soft succulent fruit.

Up here on the hill, there is tranquillity itself. It's as if we have arrived in Heaven. Old men compete against themselves and with each other in a friendly, helpful, cooperative kind of way, trying to produce the most perfect, large, spherical, brightly coloured Chrysanthemum and the most flavoursome vegetables. They rejoice in each others successes and share growing secrets and give each other tips and advice and share tools and cuttings and knowledge.

The same men compete to grow celery and gooseberries and strawberries under glass. These men share a vision of Heaven and they have created their vision here on Earth. Most have seen the depth of man's inhumanity to man in one or both of the World Wars. They are brave, intrepid men. They don't have great wealth but they are wealthy beyond limit, for they are the meek who are in the process of inheriting the Earth.

Looking beyond towards the horizons, you will see farms out on the very fringes of civilisation, farms bordering the Turbaries and wilds. These farms are administered only in flickering candle light, for there has never been electricity supplied to these farms, or any of their communes. Some are poor farms, with poor animals, often badly built outhouses and some with very poor soil but this is a time when you can farm badly and still make good money.

Some of the farms are on the fringe in every way. Some survive in a constant haze of whiskey. Eggs are sometimes left uncollected for days, cows unmilked, weeds left to seed. Hand rolled cigarettes are stuck to bottom lips and tongues are browned.

This is the age of modest rations being plenty. After the long war years, when food was really tight, even on the farms people got used to making do with very little. Now with more food and more money around, even adequate supplies seem like great bounty and the change of motivation has taken its toll on productivity on some farms.

There's a casual air in this village — there always has been but in these shadow years after the war, things are even more laid back.

Door keys are left under door mats and plant pots — they always have been, least ways by people who actually have door keys. Nothing is ever stolen. There's nothing really to steal and besides, nobody would want to steal — they wouldn't want what anyone else has got and they couldn't cope with the shame if ever they were caught.

Whirlwind's farm is right at the very top of the hill. Cherry Tree Farm enjoys the most fantastic views. Not one stick of straw has ever been allowed to roll free in this stack yard. No yard has ever been kept cleaner. No one has ever worked harder. No weed has ever been allowed to show in these lands.

Whistle Wood

10. The Trossocks to Church Town

At this point we must decide to turn left or right. Left takes us down Crook Hill whereas right takes us over the top to the blackness of Church Town. We'll head to Church Town now over the Trossocks. We'll return to this very spot and head down Crook Hill after dinner.

There are few houses over the Trossocks for these are wild lands. The land is exposed and the houses such as they are, are subject to storms and bad weather. Pog lives on his own in a small house over this way. He spends his day retired, playing the organ and touching his music with a pencil. He was a school teacher in his working days but lived and still lives and breathes the community as all professional people do in these days. They follow the market price of clean store potatoes and the price per pound of the meats both in dead weight and on the hoof, just like those in the village whose livelihoods depend on them. In this way people who serve the community have a direct understanding of its fabric; the challenges, the desires, the needs, the ups and downs, the longing, the hopes and dreams, the struggle, the despair.

Now Pog leads a more sedate life but he still provides a valuable link between schooling and the community and of course the church. He still helps out in the school when there is illness and on Sundays he plays the organ in the church. He even bakes cakes for Mr Jangles, the Vicar for these are times when people do what they can do to help the community thrive. Everyone is needed and almost everyone contributes in a quiet civilised dignified fashion, not in despair or under any kind of pressure but quietly, with respect and compassion and tolerance and understanding.

Further on towards Church Town and the land becomes even more exposed. This is a ridge and to each side the land falls away. There is little or no shelter here and the wind howls constantly over this rolling landscape. This is the location of one of the wildest farms on the Isle. Old Walt Chugabug farms here. That's not his real name but it's the nearest that any one can get to the true pronunciation. He was sent here as a displaced person in the war from Poland to a camp in the village and settled here after the war ended to grow strong dark cabbages. He has a wife but nobody ever sees her although people say she too was from Eastern Europe and found her way here by way of displacement. Walt keeps a huge collection of vicious half breed Alsatian dogs. They are wild looking animals with frightening, howling barks. Some have manes of bristled orange hair ruffed up around their thick shoulders and running down their backs. Walt walks amongst them oblivious to their menace with a soggy brown, hand rolled cigarette stuck to his bottom lip. It's a miracle that it still smoulders in the damp. Walt is immune to the ferocity of the dogs but he's the only one who is.

Postman Percy 'Pussycat' Pearson, Welshman, (good at singing, bad at lying,) sneaks by in his slippers, pushing his bicycle as quietly as he can in a vain effort to get past without the dogs hearing him. Many of the dogs are chained up but their chains are about a hundred yards long or more. Once you hear the links of the chains reeling out you know you are in real big trouble. Within seconds a ferocious wolf will burst through the six foot high hedge and will rip a hole in your shoulder with snarling, ripping fangs.

Some of the dogs, the most ferocious, are on much shorter chains, fastened to their heavy, railway carriage, wheel-less kennels but this doesn't stop them. It merely serves to slow them down a bit. They simply drag their kennels along and are quite capable of pulling them all the way down the road as they strain to rip apart passers by limb from limb.

Come on now. We must swallow heavily and take our lives into our hands. Run but run quietly before they get us! Hopefully if they come out they'll get Pussy first. Just don't look into the yard, avoid eye contact at all costs and keep on the far side of the road and keep running as fast and as quiet as you can.

There's the sound of running and of heavy gasping.

Gradually the narrow lane tapers down a long, steady incline which helps with the running. Eventually we reach the blackness of Church Town. We won't stay here long but it's important that we see the church because Whistlewood doesn't have a church of its own and this is the focal point of much that is important in people's lives hereabouts.

11. Black Town Church Town

Some people come to church every Sunday. Some come several times a week. Others only ever come three times in their entire lives, when they are baptised, when they get married and when they die. Most come at Christmas and at Easter and at Harvest Festival for these are the big occasions in the church calendar. The majority of people attend church each and every Sunday.

People are aware of the sanctity of life and of the miracle of being. There are so many things unknown about life and death but some things seem certain - God must want you to live your life, otherwise you might just fast forward through to the good lives, if there is more than one. Also there must be reason to live a less than perfect life because no life is perfect. Although there are differences in beliefs, the church remains central to the community.

It is a most beautiful church as such ancient churches always are. It is beautifully crafted in fine, cream, honey coloured, butterscotch stone with knave and chancel and impressive arches and buttresses as rightfully befits a place of worship and prayer. It is living testament to the ingenuity and endeavour of distant generations who built it and to the high esteem in which every generation since has clearly held the church because they've kept it in such fine order for those who came after them.

Here some of the most important words heard in peoples' lives are spoken...

Vicar:
"With these words...
With this ring...
In sickness...
and in health...
From ashes to ashes...
From dust to dust."

The smell of fresh pine in this place is enough to strike dread into the bravest soul. The sacred smell of ancient oak provides more comfort. But what of that taste of dust?

Old women cast runes in their minds and weep inside for lost husbands. Some old men are left wanting, served by wives for years and then abandoned suddenly in old age when their reliance is total and their ability to look after themselves is minimal. Many of them have never washed clothes or cooked a meal in their entire long existences.

Only in the church yard do the guests sleep contented and even some of them have their grievances. You can almost hear some of the old men moaning as they lie there in eternity, parched, dying for a drink.

This church, like all old churches stands damp with tears - different kinds of tears. Tears for weddings, happiness, sadness, hope. Something final, something lost, something disappointing; dreams are made and shattered in equal measure for some of those who marry and for others who can only observe. Love and love's dreams, rainbow dawn and rainbow dreams; love is beauty no one could ever quite believe.

But life goes on, despite the miracle and callousness of fate, just like the remnants of every wedding, just like every death is endured and dealt with from within.

The 'next-day-pigeons' search through the wet confetti on the pavement outside the church. Scraps of uncooked rice are snatched. Empty bottles and broken crisps are strewn on the pavement like clumsy remarks. If only more could be done for the vulnerable, the loneliness of togetherness, the constant isolation, the struggle. Such is the all consuming quest for balance, trying to acquire furniture, clothes and food in appropriate measure. Who bought them what, mouths to be fed, spoons to be used only when the vicar is round and spoons to be used when he's not. And all to be cleaned and put away in the right drawers. And the right drawers to be bought and cleaned and mended and replaced, as and when required.

Angels hover about the church. Here touchstones and candled prayers float serenely about the alter. Candles are lit and prayers are whispered into them. The Bible promised truths, the courts have heard but not believed; are lived out by the people daily. It is an echo of dawn. Everyone knows the day breaks every morning but few ever care to experience it or acknowledge its presence. Somehow these things are easier to ignore. Let's hope that God and the angels understand.

Then there are the tears for the recent dead, before too many tides have come back and forth, whilst the loss is still raw.

Nearby in 'the Church Hall' is the place where all manner of meetings are held including the monthly council meeting. It was here in 1947 that the local council, sick of war time rationing and shortages, got a bit ahead of themselves and passed the 'Bananas For The People Act.' It was never quite clear where all the bananas were to come from but no one ever got to find out because it wasn't long before the act was hastily repealed.

Whistle Wood

The Church Yard

Inevitably old people dwell on death in these surrounds and in the church yard. The place exudes reverence and commands respect. Everyone knows that once they fail, once their heart misses that very last beat, they will take their place in this yard. Each death is discussed, considered and cross examined to make sure it can be real.

Old Woman1:

"She should never have died."

Old Woman2:

"If only she'd taken the pills."

Old Woman1:

"Who would have thought?"

Old Woman2:

"Just a fish bone."

Old Woman1:

"That's all it was."

Old Woman2:

"And what a fine, big woman she was too."

Old Woman1:

"And poor Martha as well. She died of bad wrinkles on a terrible foggy night."

In death people expect some compassionate words from the vicar about ashes and dust and such like, then plenty of sandwiches and a few pints in the Joiners' Arms public house, the finest ham and the freshest bread - not that they'll be seeing any of it. But at least it provides some certainty.

Whether there will be an eternal heavenly paradise, they'll have to wait to find out but at least as they lay on their death beds they can be content in the knowledge there will always be some sandwiches and plenty of beer in the Joiners' to commemorate their passing. There may even be an inquest by a coroner. There'll definitely be an inquest by the village women.

There will also be words committed to stone and something similar wrote in the local paper...

Old Woman1:

"In dear memory."

Old Woman2:

"Much missed."

Old Woman1:

"Died of very bad luck. Very bad indeed. And such a lovely woman. Who would have thought? Who indeed? An accident of drowning – a case of too much water in the whiskey."

Some graves are marked with aphorisms both real and amended...

Old Woman1:

"Out of site *(sic)* but never out of mind."

Old Woman2:

"Absence makes the heart grow fonder."

Other graves are marked with defiance of personalities and the way they were regarded by others, as if to make the most of this last chance to put down some last enduring words...

Old Woman1:
"Falsely accused of falsehood."

Graves betray the last crumblings of the last faded, powdered writing for these poor lost souls. But how sorry are we to feel? Surely their pain is over and they will rest forever in deep, undisturbed bliss of eternal heavenly paradise. At least they can never be killed again.

Some old men lie in the graveyard smiling. They lie with an eternal belly full of bacon and blisters but they are having the last laugh for they no longer have to endure any pain. Other old men lie there dying for a drink slumbering in eternal thirst. Young men, who will never feel the pain of old age, lie beside them, all just six feet under but deep enough to be isolated from the crash and bang of the still living.

A young girl drowned, lies holding her whip and top and hugs her three babies who were never born – all of them lovely looking girls as well.

Farmers who once dug the land now lie within it. The geometry of the grave yard scares some as they try to envisage where their place must be. It's like the layout of a school classroom, it can appear random but to some there is some kind of underlying order.

The parsimonious lay amongst the generous now, all of them equally dispossessed, reduced and stripped of their Earthly wealth and life's vital signs. Motor cycle deaths, victims of farm machinery, lightening, bad luck and flawed medical practice, lie in some other shared, collective conscience. The village dogs can hear the creaking bones of the "nearly dead" and howl at the thought of all those bones lying unchewed in their coffins.

An apple tree grows in the grave yard. It is hung heavy with lush golden fruit from the previous year that no one ever touches; our very own 'Eden' with our very own sacred fruit.

The worst deaths attract the most of the consideration amongst the village gossips. Some are remembered for years.

Old Woman1:

"He died of kippers."

Old Woman2:

"Barely forty nine."

Old Woman1:

"Very unfortunate."

Old Woman2:

"Bad kippers."

Old Woman1:

"Very bad kippers."

Old Woman2:

"They were on his breath."

P.J. Naughton

Old Woman1:

"They found them swimming in his lungs."

Old Woman2:

"Third rate kippers, eaten in a second rate establishment."

For some their most remarkable parts of their lives have come about in death. Jupiter Roberts had the most memorable record in this graveyard - he died twice. In 1956 at the age of sixty three he was declared dead but despite all the odds and against the best advice of the medical practitioners, he made a remarkable recovery. The second time around he wasn't so lucky. In the summer of 1959 he succumbed for the second and final time. Some thought he might even rise again, some even took bets on it but they were to be disappointed. He might be the only man in Britain with two grave stones.

One poor old man had the dubious honour of having to stand at his own funeral. The vicar decided to take pity on the village drunk and employed him for a while as the grave digger, in the hope of rehabilitating him. Turbo dug a grave a full twelve inches too short. No one noticed until it was too late. They ended up having to stand the coffin up in the hole whilst they went ahead with the service. Turbo claimed somebody had cut a foot off his tape measure but nobody was convinced, certainly not the vicar and as a result Turbo's career as a grave digger was very short lived. Others died in way befitting the way they lived.

Old Woman1:

"He coughed up his liver see."

Old Woman2:

"And his brains."

Old Woman1:

"And his lungs."

Old Woman2:

"And his kidneys."

Old Woman1:

"And several of his vital organs."

Old Woman2:

"But he never coughed up his heart. He held on to that."

Old Woman1:

"That was Stanley, he was always the romantic."

Old Woman2:

"He coughed up a full bowl of cherries though."

Old Woman1:

"Well I never."

Old Woman2:

"The doctor said they were Amaretto but I was never certain."

The doctor's surgery lies uncomfortably close, just a few short paces down from the grave yard. Dr Silus feels distinctly uneasy whenever he passes by the church as he inevitably must do on a daily basis, you see the churchyard is filled with many of his worst professional mistakes. His embarrassment is palpable as gradually more and more of the vacant spaces have been consumed. When he isn't trying to save lives, the good doctor is out on the fields with his gun killing bird life. All that fresh air makes his consumption worse but at least in his leisure his killing is intentional, he seems to gain something of comfort from this. His surgery is filled with so many dead birds each of them stuffed and set in glass cases, as if they might spring back to life in some miraculous way like old Jupiter and escape. At least he can look back in some relief at that particular mistake, for once the outcome was a life not lost albeit by total accident. Mostly he has very little time for his patients. Mostly he says they aren't as badly as him. Mostly he's right.

The Ancient Hood

Immediately outside the church is the stone where the ancient game of the Hood is marked each year. The story of t'Hood is handed down mainly by word and mouth. Tradition has it that hundreds of years ago the Lady of the Manor was riding across the land when her hood blew off. Thirteen labourers were working in a nearby field. The man who caught the hood, the fool, was too shy to hand the hood back, so he threw it up for his twelve work mates to fight over; to win the honour of handing the hood back to the Lady.

The Lady enjoyed the spectacle so much that she insisted that the game be repeated annually every year since then on the 6th January, the last day of Christmas. The day starts fairly early with a traditional English breakfast and whisky in one of the local pubs. The Hood party then go on a tour of the other local pubs. There's lots of singing and drinking. The fool is smoked on a stone outside the church early in the afternoon of the sixth before the procession moves off on to local fields.

There, twelve boggins act as marshals and a Lord and Chief Boggin referee the proceedings. The children compete for twelve sacking hoods. Any child getting one of these hoods past the boggins and back to a local pub is rewarded with a small cash prize. The main Hood is wrapped in a leather cylinder. It is thrown up amongst the locals who compete in a massive sway, a crowd sometimes of many hundreds of people, each trying to push the Hood to their favourite local pub.

Lord Of The Hood:

"Hoose agee-anst Hoose.

Toon agee-anst Toon,

If tha' meets a man,

knock 'im doon,

but do-an't 'ut 'im."

Over the years, properties have been protected with sand bags, old women have used hose pipes, walls have been pushed over, cars and even buses have been picked up and carried or turned over. The traditional folklore songs have been sung times without number — "John Barley Corn", "To Be A Farmers Boy"...etc.

Drunken men, from all walks of life, have played their part in countless Hoods. Soldiers, drunken women, drunken horses, drunken dogs - they've all played their part.

Way beyond Church Town you eventually come to the river Trent and the wild docks. Uncertain looking migrants ride mysterious barges pulling through the tides and darkness up and down the river. Tales of floods and the Aegir, the river bore and men lost overboard in mysterious circumstances, rumours of gambling and heavy drinking and smuggling are exchanged in hushed whispers. Stories of tides so heavy that houses were washed away and rumours that men could move anything for the right price of course are passed down. At the head of the river is another place; Treacle Town beyond which is another world which most inhabitants of the Isle have never bothered to set foot into and never will.

Whistle Wood

12. Back O'er The Hill.

Turning back to Whistlewood we head up over the hill along 'Low Road' back to the pub for lunch. There are no houses here, just large swathes of traditional strip land and cabbages until we get back over the hill into the village. Spot the water tower high up on the brow of the hill as we pass. This edifice feeds the entire area with water pumped up from the aquifers on the outskirts of the village.

Further a field, just before the horizon you can just make out Twanker's Gorge where most boys learn to smoke.

Over by Sugar Plumb's, the recycled bicycle merchant; past Paddy Jackson's and her Earthquake daughters and steeply down into the village; past "teapot cottage"; past Mr Abstinence and past the smell of fresh paint from his freshly painted, shiny, ever pristine Second World War, electric green, oil dripping lorry; dripping clearly and methodically like an expensive carriage clock, into a shining drip tray;

past the smell of leather from the cobblers, (dead cow beaten into shoes and wallets,) past the Methodists; past the wall paper shop; past the junk shop; past the other councillor's and down the other hill and finally back to the Joiners' for our well earned ale and sandwiches. If you are lucky there won't be a funeral on and you'll get a seat. Otherwise you'll get free sandwiches but if they were popular, you might find you have to stand.

13. A Pub Lunch

Outside, across the road from the pub door, Acorn Harris is talking to Chestnut Dawson. Mint Johnson stands nearby trying to bring the conversation to an end, or at least move it nearer towards the pub. Mint is parched. He's only forty nine years old but looks more like ninety, probably because he smokes so profusely. He looks like a pickled walnut and is even the same colour. All the moisture has been drained from his body. He works in a nearby brickyard in one of the neighbouring villages but he's still back there on the Burma railway somewhere, still struggling to survive, else struggling in the freezing night cold, Atlantic sea of oil. He had a difficult war for such a young man, seeing action both on the high seas in the merchant navy then in India where he suffered terribly as a prisoner of war at the hands of the Japanese. He hasn't been able to shake off his experiences or to put them behind him. To be blessed in this way, what kind of God do we have to have?

As we walk in through the pub door, we are met by clouds of billowing smoke, the sight of the fire comes and goes. The chimney must be blocked again, probably birds nests but nobody cares. This is Whistle's answer to Brown's of Laharne. You're in luck. There's no funeral today so you'll have no bother finding a seat.

Men stand at the bar, eager for beer, as dry as a budgies cage. No beer could slake their thirst except the beer of the Joiners', from the bright frothy orange to the dark, solid, cellar stout.

These people are in tune with nature. They are used to wood fires, smoke and the smell of bacon cooking. It's the way people have always lived. This pub, along with all the other pubs in the region, sells the range of beers which farming communities need to oil the cogs of the seasons. Oily dark beer, stout, full of dark secrets from a dark world, home to clawed sea horses, the half dead caught half way between life and death, bumping and swaying in the infinite vat of hops and bubbles, hopeless paradise where nothing can ever change to break the monopoly of perfection and yet somehow it did, we let it and somehow all this slipped away.

Mr Barlow, journalist on one of the local papers is already drunk. It's just as well, this way he'll forget most of what he hears in conversation. The editor and printer of the paper comes from a nearby village. He's also usually drunk and it shows in his work. So much of the print is upside down and back to front. Even Bletchley Park couldn't decipher some of these stories. Luckily, many of the village locals can not read and therefore never even notice. They appear to be the majority who buy the newspaper each week. For the others, the quality of type setting adds to the discussion.

Cuckoo Walters:

"Did you see that about ...?"

Jock:

"Terrible!"

Cuckoo Walters:

"It was disgusting."

Jock:

"And so badly punctuated and all."

Someone is thumbing the pages of last week's edition, stories from a drunken village typed by a drunken man. Prices of cattle sold dead and alive are mixed with news of births, marriages and deaths, in the crazy mixed up pages of this local newspaper. Stories of trials and tribulations are written out, clouds above the heads of local people– clouds we all must get from time to time. It's all part of the fabric of the Earth, the natural cycle of life - birth and death, marriage, survival, struggle, endeavour. Here amongst the words that are wrote, the words that were spoke and the words that are heard, there's a report that Ambrose Carter won the annual wheel barrow race.

Women are always addressed in print by their husbands' names. 'Mrs Percy Smith won the tombola, Mrs Stanley Garter got the prize for the best decorated doyley'.

Children are always referred to by the eldest sibling's name of the same sex – one name per family, saves on a lot of remembering.

There's also news of a wedding. It was a big do. This is the height of the marriage season. The article lists all details of the ceremony, who was present, the sandwich fillings, the colour of the dress.

Mau:

"She wore yellow!"

Lulu:

"The shame."

Not everyone was invited. Old Mr Mustard is seated drinking jet, black stout. He didn't get an invite. People are astonished. He's the bride's great Uncle. He closes one eye to light his pipe before explaining about it all to Lulu the bee-hived land lady.

Mr Mustard:

"It was a posh do – they didn't invite us cos we'd start supping pints and saying things like, 'How much?'"

Lulu:

"Have they gone away?"

Mr Mustard:

"Aye, they're in Therpes for the week. He'll be grunting like a buffalo, coupling, you know!"

Lulu:

"It might kill him what with his heart."

Mr Mustard:

"At least he'd die with a smile on his lips. Bozz eyed though."

Mr Mustard is putting a brave face on it all but Lulu can see that he's hurt. She uses her wiles as a bar maid in an attempt to lighten the mood.

P.J. Naughton

Lulu:

"Where are you going for your holidays?"

Mr Mustard:

"No where. What about you?"

Lulu:

"I'm off to Therpes next year – early on like - in March."

Mr Mustard is not impressed.

Mr Mustard:

"Therpes? In March?"

Lulu:

"It'll be a bit cheaper."

Mr Mustard:

"Aye it'll be cheap alright – it'll be shutten."

There's excitement at the bar, talk of yet more nuptials. This time Dolly Daydream (real name Susan) is getting wed again. She's twenty seven year old. She's had three husbands and five children, all by different fathers. The young woman, heavily pregnant, is standing at the bar, waiting in the pub for her fourth wedding to start – supping pints, head dress beside her feet in a plastic 'Next' carrier bag.

Lulu:

"She's about to start on her fourth husband."

Mr Mustard:

"She's just about to hatch her sixth child."

Lulu:

"Is it his?"

Mr Mustard:

"I don't know. Nobody does but the last one looked like the milkman."

P.J. Naughton

Lulu:

"Sssh, she's coming over."

Dolly walks over to Lulu and Mr Mustard.

Lulu:

"Hello Susan you do look lovely."

Mr Mustard:

"What are you having?"

Dolly:

"A pony!"

Mr Mustard:

"I thought so!"

Dolly:

"Won't be a minute, just need the loo."

Dolly goes off to visit the bathroom.

Lulu:

"Really! Couldn't she have asked for a Babycham."

Mr Mustard:

"Aye, she could 'ave."

Lulu:

"Or just another pint of stout?"

Mr Mustard:

"Who's she marrying this time?"

Lulu:

"Pearling's lad."

Mr Mustard:

"What young Tom? He's nowt but a lad. He can't be more than fourteen."

Lulu:

"That's what I've heard."

Mr Mustard:

"He won't last 'til Christmas."

Lulu:

"He won't last until next Friday."

Mr Mustard:

"It'll be like chucking a sausage down our street."

Lulu:

"Waggling a pencil in a bucket of water."

On the way back from the toilet Dolly meets her friend Podge and starts chatting to him. In Dolly's eyes she thinks of herself as respectable, sophisticated even. Her tattoos are spelled right and she nearly always says 'pardon' when she farts. She sees herself as the Liz Taylor of Whistle but the tides of time have left their mark. Podge is as thin as a rake, exceptionally tall, clothed in dark blue badly stained overalls and oil and grease.

Podge and Dolly pal on like brother and sister. Both have stains on their character. In these times women generally only ever go into pubs on Boxing Day evening or when they are widowed in old age, at which time the daily consumption of Milk Stout becomes part of their accepted life style. Dolly is unusual in ignoring this convention. Podge has a different shadow to contend with. There was once a theft from a local house in the village. There were no visible signs of a break in, all the doors and windows were locked and there was no evidence of a forced entry. It was rumoured that Podge must have crept under the door, took the money and crept out again. He was the only one thin enough to get in through a gap like that.

A small crowd, in amongst the throng are talking about the imminent marriage.

Podge:

"Aren't women lucky? If ever they want to sniff cheese in the night all they need to do is lean over and smell the feet of the man lying next to them."

Dolly takes the bait.

Dolly:

"But cheese smells awful. Who'd want to smell cheese?"

Jock:

"Oh you will my dear. You just have to find the right flavour. Take Adam here. He's more your mature Gorgonzola."

Mr Mustard draws heavily on his pipe.

Mr Mustard:

"I'm more your smoked Cheddar. Perhaps more to your taste my dear?" (...he suggests hopefully.)

Elsewhere in the pub the usual topics of conversation are rehearsed yet again as they have been since time in memorial. As you might expect in an agricultural area, the weather is discussed in detail. Each and every rain shower is analysed.

Whistle Wood

Old Adam:

"We had lightening over Home Farm last Monday."

Mr Mustard:

"We had it an' all."

Old Adam:

"It didn't give thunder."

Mr Mustard:

"They never do."

Tips for horse races you'll never hear any more about are exchanged. As the lunchtime thickens and the ale continues to flow, some of the conversations become less prosaic.

Old Adam:

"There's been a murder."

Mr Mustard:

"Have they found a body?"

Old Adam:

"No there's no body."

Mr Mustard:

"Well has any one gone missing?"

Old Adam:

"No, nobody has gone missing."

Mr Mustard:

"Well how do they know there's been a murder then?"

Old Adam:

"That's where they've been clever. But it'll be their undoing, just mark my words."

Mr Mustard is looking into a dry glass now as if to see his future. At least he's wet on the inside.

Dolly is casting around in anxiety, trying to seek out the time. The pub clock has been stuck at midday (or midnight depending on your point of view,) for the best part of the last twenty years, ever since Lulu's husband Ken passed away. Most of the old men have pocket watches. Some aren't wound. A number of different times are proposed. Eventually Dolly decides it's time to set off for her latest wedding. Her friend Diadora kisses her on her tight lips and wishes her good luck. Diadora is helping Lulu out and there's plenty to be done what with the sandwiches to be cut and everything. She helps out "serving on" in the village bar. The rewards are meagre but it helps to make ends meet.

Dolly is accompanied to this wedding by Jock's daughter 'Tattoo McDonald', fair of face, foul of mouth, who is acting as Dolly's second/corner man/woman on this occasion. Mr Mustard is interested to know whether Tattoo is getting herself fixed up as well.

Mr Mustard:

"Is tha getting wed?"

Jock answers on her behalf. There's real disappointment in his voice...

Jock:

"Neah. They've stalled."

Of course Dolly's do is at a Registry Office, she's chosen the place in Toffee Town near the Gaumont because it's handy for the buses if anybody wants to come. But she's going in style, Tattoo is driving her. She'll take the opportunity to call into the nursing home of her grandfather to show him the latest ring. She'll drop off a few bottles of nutmeg brown ale, the finest milk stout. She has to couple a rubber teat on a bottle for him to drink out of since he had his last stroke last Winter but he still enjoys his drink.

One of the farmers is explaining to Jock about a recent fire he suffered in his yard.

Farmer Fudge Brown:

"All that work, the water and firemen and it cost nowt."

Jock:

"Well it's paid for out of your taxes. You do pay your taxes don't you Mester?"

The local Bobby draws up at the pub on his 49cc Puch Maxi moped. There are laws about drinking but they're widely ignored by many of the locals. Inevitably conversation in the pub turns to the matters of crime that are reported in the local paper.

Mr Mustard:

"Pie-eyed Harris has been done again I see."

Jock:

"What was it this time?"

Mr Mustard:

"No rear reflector and drunk in charge of a bike."

Jock:

"Was the Judge drunk?"

Mr Mustard:

"I'd think so."

It's widely thought that the 'weighing scales' of justice need to be replaced with a spinning bottle and a dice about these parts.

Mr Mustard:

"Peggy was called upon to tell the truth, the whole truth and nothing like the truth."

Jock:

"She never?"

Mr Mustard:

"She did an' all!"

The shared thought of the abstainers on the bench scowling, cause the old men to chuckle. There's history between the 'Pledge givers' and the imbibers.

PC Green comes in, removes his helmet and picks up on the conversation.

PC Green:

"The magistrate struggled to grasp the circumstances through that thick fog of liquor he's always got about him."

The Court Room

Magistrate:

"Three years!"

Barrister:

"But we haven't heard the evidence yet."

Magistrate:

"Twelve months then."

Barrister:

"The lottery of justice."

The magistrate struggles to focus on the papers which he holds in his hands.

Magistrate:

"Arrested for being drunk? Outrageous."

Barrister:

"Remember sir, you are sentencing the drinker."

Magistrate:

"Oh am I? Five shillings then."

Pie-Eyed is relieved because he's appeared in this courtroom so many times before and he'd been expecting the worst.

Pie-Eyed:

"Thank you sir, I'll see to it yeah'll have a good drink on me."

And so justice is dispensed and the world is set to right, the checks and balances are adjusted and the people can rest once more at ease in their beds; certain that justice has been served.

Back In The Pub...

The pub oven has given up its batch of warm meat pies and like Lulu the landlady, is still dripping with the warmth but is gradually beginning to cool. Men in a hurry; farmers on a mission, have already been in and had a pie and a pint and are back on their way back to the day's toil. The crowd is beginning to thin. Lulu is visibly more relaxed. She's got through the worst of the lunchtime rush once again and is going through her daily ritual of boasting to anyone who might listen.

Lulu:

"I look after the pub all on my own you know."

P.J. Naughton

Not everyone is impressed. Mr Mustard hisses to an old man sitting nearby.

Mr Mustard:

"She's always like this. The toilet floor must be four inches deep and there's been no handle on the flush for at least eleven years that I can remember."

But no one would dare raise one word of open dissent for fear of being barred. The pub holds a near monopoly position in the village and to get barred could prove costly. You see the old method of strip farming is still practised here in the village. The 'Mares' (strips of land about five yards wide and perhaps half a mile long) are 'auctioned' off annually in the pub in the Autumn. Pins are pushed into a lighted candle. Bids are made for each patch of land and the last person to make a bid before a pin falls out of the candle wins a 'Mare' for the year for a nominal sum of a few shillings. 'Mares' are hotly contested. Not only are the pieces of land highly valued in their own right but with luck it can be possible to inherit someone else's crop if they have been remiss and say left a length of leeks or swedes in place, gambling perhaps that they might win their 'Mare' back for another year. So everyone watches their 'p's' and 'q's' and Lulu wields a certain amount of power and is well aware of this. Gradually the lunchtime crowd is melting away. Time to finish our drinks and drift back outside.

The Coop

Opposite the pub, Mr Wright the manager of the village Coop is serving Mrs Victor who is having a very bad day...

Mrs Victor:
"I want a box of matches."

Mr Wright:
"But you don't smoke."

Mrs Victor:
"No, I'm going to set the world on fire."

The range of goods in the shop is perfunctory. There's everything anyone would need to survive but very little else. Exotic vegetables in this time are potatoes brought from the next village. Flowers are hung and dried but rarely bought. There'll be a wedding soon, or a baby, then they'll be needed. Someone is getting a bunch of lilies though. Who cares that they aren't spelt right.

Oysters from the wet fish man are displayed in this shop for them who missed him on his round. Moist women poke and haggle and moan over a bag of danglers and a bunch of monkey fruit. Clouds drift across the village. They come and go. Most are unnoticed.

Outside at the bus stop, older youths are waiting for a bus on their way to the local swimming pool in a nearby village to pick up a verruca, well it's something to take to the doctors. We've been offered a lift in the back of a pickup, back to the top of Candy Hill, where we'll pick up our tour of the village again.

Whistle Wood

14. Drifting Down Crook Hill

One wave from Old Walt in the wing mirror of his pickup and he pulls away, full of strawberries and beef, in a cloud of blue smoke, leaving us back at the pinnacle of Candy Hill. Last time we were here, we turned right and headed off to Church Town but this time we'll turn left and drift down the ever so tranquil Crook Hill. Here, the hedgerows are thick with blossom and pungent wild flowers of every shade.

Upon the hill, behind us, a terrible squealing is going on. Chuck Richards is trying to kill a pig in his yard with a blunt poker. He started off the killing wearing a cowboy hat with feathers in it. Now it's the pig who is squealing round the yard with the hat on. Chuck needs the bacon. He spends his working life spreading muck on the land. For most farmers muck spreading is a few weeks in November after the last of the harvest and before the hardest frosts but to Chuck it's his life time.

Every morning, he wakes up at the crack of dawn and goes straight outside to fire up his tractor. He then leaves it to warm up whilst he goes back inside to eat his breakfast. He's certainly got plenty of bacon. The killing of a pig brings a lot of benefits. Nothing is wasted except the squeal.

Just a little way down the hill we come across Boris the taxi man. He's drunk again, so is his imaginary friend Stan.

Visitor:

"Hello! Pleased to meet you."

Boris:

"How do?"

Visitor:

"Very well thank you. How are you?"

Boris:

"I'm normal. And so is my brother, Stan."

Some say there's too much salt in the aquifers about these parts – that accounts for a lot of what goes on. It encourages the thirst.

Children plait flowers amongst the nettles and herbs on the grassy banks. They should be in school really. Daisy chains are strewn across the lane. Children wait in anticipation for a car or tractor to come along to sweep through the chains. They have to have a lot of patience about these parts. Sometimes the chains of flowers can remain unbroken all afternoon. The place is an absolute paradise. It's hard to believe that many men from this village fought in Burma just twenty five years previously.

Jim The Sailor

Jim the old sailor is standing on his doorstep, smoking. He's unsure on his legs, like he still has the ocean swaying beneath his feet. The salt of the sea is in his blood, gushing beneath his leathered skin. He knows more about magic and treasure, dark nights and mutiny than any one else in the village. He holds on to all his memories despite his very advanced age. His memories are precious but he lives alone. He always has done. In quiet moments he can't help thinking back, remembering how he pulled himself from an oily ocean after his torpedoed frigate crumbled beneath his feet. But he carries an unjustified sense of guilt. He's ridden the heaving seas which many men have failed to survive. He's ended up with a belly full of ulcers and brought tattoos back from distant lands and exotic diseases the doctors have never seen before. Salt and rum flow through his veins.

Mr Harris Smith lives next door to old Jim in the adjoining semi-detached house. Carpenter, doctor, poet, solicitor, habitual liar. He's been everywhere, done everything, seen it all. The only thing really known for sure about him is that his name is neither Harris nor Smith. He claims he was once a writer but nobody has ever seen anything he ever wrote. But as he is always quick to explain, all writing eventually ends up in the same place.

Harris Smith:

"The writer throws away at least half of it, the publisher throws away the other half. The rest gets printed and when it's been read by the public, what's left is thrown away. Sometimes, (although rarely) a book is kept on a shelf to gather dust for a few years. This achievement is the reserve of the most successful writers. It is the very highest accolade a writer can aspire to. But invariably these books end up not being sold at a jumble sale and are finally thrown away."

It seems all our life's endeavours finally end up on a 'tidy tip'. But then I suppose that very prospect isn't exclusively reserved for writers.

Whistle Wood

Old Jim:

(shouting through the partition...)
"All that waste paper wasted on walls and writing. It's now't but a crime really."

Mr Harris, (or should it be Smith?) is sucking a pencil and conjugating verbs.

Harris Smith:
"I'm in love. She's in love. They are in love."

Old Jim:
"Here's to broken voices."

Harris Smith:
"... and fallen women."

Old Jim:
"...and to broken dreams and broken sleep."

Harris Smith:
"...and broken marriages and broken shop windows."

Old Jim:

"Here's to broken ..."

Harris Smith:

"Go to sleep!"

Old Jim:

"...broken verse."

Harris Smith:

"...and broken bones."

Colin the milkman, lost in a dream, is drifting along behind his herd of cows, past Old Jim's front door, down Crook Hill, drunk on the fragrance of blossom. His thoughts are in poetry. The cows crop casually from the flowered banks as they amble along. Hours late for the early morning, milking is supposed to take place at the crack of dawn but no one cares, not even the cows. This ritual is repeated daily. It's what they know – it's what they're used to.

Mrs Brown

Old Mrs Brown is the face at the next window going down the hill. The fumes of Mrs Brown's, brown vapour kitchen, spill out down the side of the hill. She keeps at least three dozen permanent cats and many strays. They preen in pristine comfort amongst the toxic clouds of the paraffin stove and the ever present boiling of Camp coffee, made from a long list of ingredients, none of which include coffee. A cat sneezes and breathes its T.B. spores into the clouds of woodbine smoke and urine vapour which billow through the house.

The flies in the kitchen re-enact the 'Battle of Britain' and try to avoid coming to a sticky end on the brown paper fly traps that are stuck thick with flies. Flies stuck to flies. Other flies are circling their death. The overpowering zeal of camphor and moth balls, cut into the atmosphere. People of these times are frightened that moths will eat their settees. In most families, there isn't money to buy another one, so moth balls are heavily used, almost to the point of coma.

Hems are replaced, curtains are mended, trousers all shortened, on "Mrs Brown's machine" - all for the price of ten woodbines (no filter.)

Inky, Binky and Stinky, three of the blackest of cats, crouch by the open doorway. Inky flashes his claws. Binky curls his lip and bares his teeth. Stinky gorges at the feeding bowl. One black cat makes a witch. Mrs Brown is known as a triple witch by the local children. What do triple witches do? They turn you into a frog three times as fast.

The cats are praying, as much as cats can, that a Cray fish will fall off the back of the fish mongers van when he calls later this afternoon. This is indeed a very sleepy part of a very sleepy town. The cats expressions show obvious disappointment when they hear a tradesman approaching and realise it's not the fish man.

Mr Venables, money lender, fixer, loan shark, club man, the 'Never, Never man', smells as ever of whisky. He's struggling with drink. He's burnt his insides raw and scorched his mind but he's always impeccably polite and extremely well spoken and he always raises his trilby when he greets anyone.

His knock at the door costs 'half-a-crown' but it means a piece of new carpet whenever you need one or that essential new gadget that you both know you just can't afford but are determined to have anyway. It's 'half-a-crown' down and 'half-a-crown' every time Mr Venables catches you in. For most people, Mr Venables is the only access to credit apart from the slate in the Joiners' and as such he provides a much valued service. Besides, if you haven't got the money for him, you can always just buy him a drink instead. Otherwise you have to hide when you know he's coming.

No-Good Boyo and His Darling Sweetheart...

Down both sides of the hill giant ash trees stand, impressive and proud, huge thick straight trunks with huge canopies of leaves. About halfway down the hill stands the 'big tree', it isn't the tallest but it is the tree with the thickest trunk and the one that the children can easily climb and build dens in. On the side of the 'big tree' there are carvings of love, one of the most prominent was cut by 'No-Good Boyo' to his darling Grace many years ago.

No one could understand it. Why did they never get together? Perhaps it was vanity on her part or selfishness on his. He wanted children. She'd never admit to even liking him. He was scared she'd destroy him and she would have done if she'd ever left him. His early life was so bad. It wasn't something that anyone would want to share, certainly not with someone you really love. He couldn't subject her to that. Besides she was in such a rush. She left school at sixteen. He didn't leave school until he was well turned eighteen. How could everything have turned out like this?

No-Good lives in the house just across from the 'big tree' – he's lived there through out his childhood. It is the most envied location. No-Good and his small band of friends stood for hours over the years outside Mabel's store to collect discarded 'Bazooka Joe' bubblegum wrappers. Collect fifty wrappers and you can send off for a 'Bazooka Joe' spy kit, complete with flash light and code book. Children through out the village still get out of bed in the middle of each and every night to flash 'Bazooka Joe' messages to each other, that no one can ever understand.

Mr No-Good, No-Good's dad, is off work, on the sick after working hard on the land and on the roads all his life. He has a wardrobe full of shirts but only ever wears a vest. His favourite vest is full of holes. He fears the worst and has been on a strict diet for weeks, in an effort to slim down sufficiently to fit comfortably in his suit, ready to be dressed for his coffin. Mrs No-Good takes meticulous care of her beloved husband. She hand feeds him with re-warmed stew pie, mustard-mash and chocolate cake and ice cream. He always puts his best vest on to read the paper, each and every Sunday morning but he prefers the one he wears all week with the holes in.

Mrs No-Good:

"Change your vest, you might have an accident. I don't want to be visiting you in the infirmary with you in a stained vest."

Mrs No-Good gives her husband weekly baths and makes him change his vest and pants, whether he wants to or not. Bathing is a major challenge in these times.

Most people have to rely on water heated from their coal fires – systems which mostly don't work very well. A roaring fire all day long is usually just sufficient to produce a few inches of lukewarm water in the bottom of a bath. As a result, people have a pragmatic approach to hygiene. Most folk wash their hands and face each morning and hands are usually washed before each meal but it's not unusual for people to bathe only every fortnight, or even once a month.

You can smell some of the village residents coming from about a mile away but people don't care much about that as long as they are honest and truthful and reliable. These are the qualities which people genuinely respect. Indeed the odour of sweat is a sign of a hard worker, something to be admired.

'Ash cans' stand outside every house, some bright and shiny, some black and dinted. Some people call these dustbins but it seems more appropriate that they are called 'ash cans' because the only thing that ever goes in them is the ashes from the fires. All rubbish is thrown onto the fire first, even tin cans. It saves on fuel and it saves on rubbish.

The older people still remember the war years and do tend to make use of things which come their way - string, brown paper, cardboard – anything useful is meticulously wrapped and carefully stored for times when it might come in handy. That's the way people with so little, manage to make sure they have everything they need.

Every year, on the very first day of December, Mrs No-Good puts up about three hundred Christmas cards - all from people long since dead. The couple only ever receive about a dozen new cards each year but it helps to remember better years past.

Once past the half way point of the hill there's only one more house; more of a wooden hut really. Two old gypsies live there, retired and content, him carving ornaments of Red Indian chiefs all day long and painting them and giving them to passing children and her preparing the most wonderful meals for them both to enjoy. The rest of the hill is given over to pussy willow trees and wild flowers.

15. The Foot Of The Hill.

Down at the foot of Crook Hill, a group of boys are gathered at the lily pond. They too should be in school but haven't bothered or just haven't bothered to return after dinner. Some are knee deep in the water trying to catch frogs in their dinner break, even though dinner hour ended at least an hour ago.

The village pond is yet another important meeting place in the village. Dragonflies hover above the margins whilst ducks circle the pond trying to weigh up who might feed them next. The sky is thick with swallows, swifts and house martins. A lone donkey stands on wasted ground at the end of a very long rope. Charged with regret and with reflection – he'd bray but he knows he wouldn't win any response. But he is in sight of the waters of the pond. He stares deep and distant into the water and he alone can see the reflections in this way and thereby gains meaning that others rarely see. And him a modest animal without proper word and supposedly without proper thought.

In the evening, lovers meet and kiss like seals on the seat at the edge of the pond. By day, old people gather and talk to each other but some, particularly older visitors to the pond, don't always really bother to hear what others are saying to them.

Old Woman:

"What do you think the weather's going to do?"

Old Man:

"Yes I know."

Feelings are exchanged – most are hidden, others spoken in words to weave how you want to. Most are lost. For countless years since times past, old men have gathered around the village pond to witness the arrival of the first swallows on the evening of the 14th of April each year. As if by magic these wonderful birds always turn up right on schedule from their far off distant lands, followed promptly by swifts and house martins. The first swoop of the swallows is comfort of the seasons, the constant tick of time, change without change.

It seems magical that these gifted acrobatic flying marvels journey all the way back from far off foreign lands each year, to spend their Summer with the people of Whistle Wood. What made them come here in the first place? How did they decide that this was their chosen spot? How do they remember their way back over such a great distance?

At the foot of the hill are more farms. The 'Three Wisemen' farm down by the pond as does Arthur Bell. Arthur (pronounced 'Halfa' or 'Art') is a hard task master.

Halfa:

"Tha's more weeds behind thee than there is in front of thee.
Is tha' planting the buggers or what?"

Halfa has a way about him, an original way of disseminating the work ethic and of getting the most from his workforce. He always starts the week, at 6am Monday morning, by addressing his work force in the same way.

Halfa:

"Thee day at'ter tomorra is't middle o' week an' tha' an't dun nowt yet."

He's always careful to give out the instructions to the assembled workforce, to charge them up ready for the week's work. Like most farmers, Halfa has his own foibles and like the other farmers, he likes people to work the way he works. Stooking, (the standing up of sheaves of corn to dry in the fields after reaping and binding,) is a particular nervy concern for Halfa.

Halfa:

"Handle the bats carefully, the grain is very dry."

The thought of all the chickens coming on to the fields after the harvest and gorging themselves on Halfa's grain is always a sense of great frustration to him. If only he could grow a beak and peck it up himself. But this is only May. There are still many months of hard work before the harvest can begin.

Despite the direct, if primitive approach to workplace motivation, Halfa always has time to comment about international sport, especially football and the achievements of the England International side, despite never having a television or radio or ready access or any visible interest in newspapers.

Halfa:

"Fancy bloody losing to Yugo-bloody-Slovakia what dun't know bugger all aboot it."

But digressions are generally short lived. They signal to Halfa that a worker is short of something to do and after a short diversion are usually met with ...

Halfa:

"Get set to Shylock. You can work these rows."

Mrs Bell spends most of her time in an asylum in Lincoln; green ambulance, straight jacket, men in white coats with a net to catch her; the works. Some say she's depressed but it seems Art' is the one who's really depressed because he has no one to cook and do the house work and he can't do it himself. Some say she's just crackers but he's the one who's really mad. And who can blame him?

The Hooper's also farm on the rich lands at the foot of the hill. Theirs is a model farm in amongst so many excellent agricultural holdings. Cows, pigs, hens, bonfires and tractors, haystacks neatly built and carefully managed, orchards filled with glorious blossom and later thick with fruit and tatties to bake; a true paradise.

These farms, like all the farms in the area are always busy through out the year. There are always lots of jobs to be done. The working day is long. There are always eggs to collect, cows to feed and milk, yards to be swept.

Spring time is always busy with planting, singling and weeding, from early on in the year when the ground is first broken until 'turning out day' on 14th May when animals are set out on to Summer pasture after the threat of frost has finally passed. Summer starts with the hay harvest. Cutting, turning and drying, baling and leading and stacking. More than any other activity, a bad hay time can break a farm as, more than anything else, it means the survival of the animals through out the year. Summer also brings more weeding and the challenge of irrigation as the lands dry.

Late Summer brings the main harvests, fields of golden corn, potatoes, fruit to be gathered, red beet, sugar beet and mangles to be harvested well into Autumn, all to be cleaned and stored and sold. Then there are livestock markets to be attended and auctions for land and equipment.

Even the long night of Winter doesn't bring any respite. Winter brings its own jobs for farmers. There is straw to be fetched to bed the pigs, sugar beet to pulp for the cows, hay to be broken out in the byres and fold yards.

Winter brings a chance to get at the dormant land, to manage the structure and support services. There are always suff pipes to be sunk and drainage channels to be dug to deal with localised flooding, dykes to be cleaned, hedges to be cut, fences to be mended, new fence posts to be knocked in, thistles to be cut out of pasture.

Watching the farmers cut their drainage is like watching a surgeon cutting into a vein. There's always a good deal of inspection, it's the only chance they get to have a good look at what lies below the surface, what supports the surface soil which is all so very precious to them.

Getting the Christmas season right pays big dividends. A heavy snow fall in early December puts the price of sprouts up sharply, they can be the only crop farmers can get at. Those farmers who have sprouts and can find labourers to walk the land and sweep snow and frost off them and pull them, can earn good money.

Bringing stored potatoes to market at the right time, can bring similar good fortune. Growing a good crop of potatoes can be very profitable but selling them, when there are plenty of potatoes around is not the best way to maximise profits. So, many farmers store potatoes in the hope that prices will rise, later in the season. It's a risk and a balancing act, the longer you keep them, the more the quality can suffer. More of the tubers rot with time. Key to the process is sound storage.

One of the most efficient ways to store potatoes is to pie them. Potatoes are piled up in long heaps and are covered with straw and soil to keep the frost out. Later in the year when the farmers have decided the prices have optimized, they break open the pies from one end. The potatoes are then riddled, shaken through a machine to clean off the soil and stones. Labourers stand at the machines to pull off the rotten and damaged tubers. They say, "Where there's muck there's money." There's certainly money here but plenty more muck and sweat.

There's more money to be made if you are strong enough and want to go it alone. Piece work can be very profitable. That is, paid for what you achieve rather than the hours you put in. At twenty four pints of beer to the pound, it takes a very fit man 2 days to pull an acre of sugar beat and pays £10 pounds against £3.50p (equivalent) per week on wages. The prices have always been the same, ever since anyone can remember.

Turning the land is part of the way of life here. The land has changed hands so many times, mostly handed down through the generations.

Fortunes have fluctuated wildly. Most have got by, some have made good livings, others have struggled. They all struggle in one way or another. Hard work is definitely part of success but it is far from being the complete story. The weather plays its part, as does the roulette of luck. Have a plentiful crop when there are real shortages and you are a real winner. Suffering a crop failure or loss of livestock either through disease or poor management can be disastrous.

There seem to be so many more ways to fail than to succeed, so it's a real testament to the farming community, that most of the farms are a success. Some of the owners have faced so many curses, so many times. But the questions and answers all come back to the land. So many people over the generations have cropped it, run horses on it, fought over it, lived and died on it. The land is still turned after they are all gone but no more than the depth of a spade or a plough share but to the custodians, the owners, the tenant farmers and market gardeners nothing else could matter more.

It's not only the people who own the land. Foxes own it, cats and dogs own it. Even blackbirds and skylarks – even the ants and beetles all hold their claims. Farmers and ants work the fields together – mostly ignoring each others presence and even for the most part, ignoring each others labours.

Whistle Wood

16. Paradise Lane

Moving on from the wonders of the pond, we start to move back out into the countryside again, along Paradise Lane. Within a few steps the hedges thicken and grow noticeably more wild. Flowers light the way. See all the eyes watching from the hedgerows; farm animals, live stock, wild birds, cats, voles and mice - to name but a few. Large brambles hang thick with blackberry blossom and wild rose.

Blackberries are eagerly competed for in September but at this time of year people take note of where the best blossom is growing to indicate where the best fruit will be in the Autumn. Blackberries are collected avidly every year, boiled up and used to make fruit pies and wine vinegar which is bottled and drunk hot on cold Winter nights. Most of the hedgerows glow pink with the perfume of wild roses now and there's certainly no shortage of rabbit meat on Paradise Lane that's for sure. Leather bulls work the lush pastures seeking out the richest, most succulent clover and tasty wild flowers.

There are many farms down Paradise Lane but these are different farms from the others in the village. They are less well kempt, less neat, more casual and more spread out. This farming is less about model farming and more about survival. The gardens grow wild at the front of these farms and the hedges grow where they will.

Old Adam runs the first farm down Paradise Lane. He is old; very old, no one knows quite how old, not even Adam himself. He's been here donkey's years but he still carries a genuine Scottish smirk and speaks a lovely Highland brogue. He walks around with two old coats on, one over each shoulder. Recently he needed work done on his tractor. Like most farmers he only pays out when he absolutely has to. The mechanic who attended the farm had cause to use the outside toilet and had to ask Adam for some toilet roll.

Adam:

"Where's that gone now?" asked Adam with a perplexed frown.

Adam disappeared into his house and came back with an old copy of the 'Yellow Pages' which he handed over to the disbelieving mechanic.

Adam:

"I bet it was our Diadora," explained Adam. "It's now't but waste with her."

Adam keeps ducks and geese in large numbers on his farm and has a fine herd of pedigree cattle. Some say he must be a millionaire cattle breeder but you'd never know it to look at him. He's as black as an unwashed miner.

Once a pig farmer, Adam made his first real money in sheep and goats but his pedigree cows are his pride and joy now and he is known and respected far and wide, despite being a stranger to the bath tub. There is very little that he doesn't know about farming and most of the other farmers use him as a sage to help sort out their many problems, how to treat sick animals, how to improve poor land and so on.

Paradise Lane is full of corn flowers at this time of year, wild fresh corn flowers, some of unusual colours, not just the wonderful ink blue shades, although they are here in plentiful supply too. Sweet wild roses, campion, poppy, daisies, birdfoot, lilies, violets and foxgloves compete to fill the fields, hedgerows and byways. Buttercups fill the lane. They grow in the music from the fragrant green forest. Few people in this village can find the rare violets but we know where they are concealed and can enjoy their vivid fragrance when we get to them. In Autumn there will be acorns and wild apples and soft fruit hanging thick and free from these hedgerows. Skylarks compete to entertain us now as they will throughout the Summer months.

On the roadside verge, a sky lark's nest is found in the long grass by another group of boys - more boys who should be in school. None of them get much in the way of formal education but they all know what to do if a boy falls from a tree into a bunch of nettles and they all know what vetch is for. The eggs are passed between the warm hands of each and every raggy boy before being set back in the nest, stained with nicotine and ink and smelling of chocolate. By some miracle they will eventually hatch. What's that they say about a bird in the hand?

Further along from Adam's farm live the Paradise sisters, three young angels of jaw dropping beauty who landed in the village from 'God knows where.' Back on the hill Dylan groans about an Egyptian princess whilst, down here, three of them glide around these humble streets, like as if they're in some kind of living fairytale. Poetry comes easily to the lips here in this lane. Most of what is spoken comes out in rhyme. It's not called Paradise Lane for nothing.

There's the sweet smell of cawl and the Red wings fluttering in and out of the hedgerows are a constant reminder of the flag of Dyfid. Even Adam can not resist a verse...

Adam:

"Beyond those eyes,

When you stand before a mirror,

You see beyond those eyes.

you know that face you see is never you,

it's your disguise.

Everything and everyone is you.

After so many tomorrows,

the old lady with the shopping trolley and small dog,

the old man with a stick and no teeth.

They are all of them just you,

just on different days,

at different times,

in different lives.

People that are every bit of you."

Dogs are playing in the distant fields. Boys smoke and play with fires, steeped high with piles of unwanted binder-band and sacks. Hay stacks are plundered, bales are piled up to push over and castles and tunnels and towers are built. Frogs wait in swamp wasteland, waiting to be collected in boys' satchels. Wild newts seem more knowing and try to keep themselves safe in deeper water. They'll still be taken if they can be caught in the many improvised traps - various bottles and jars and nets made from wire coat hangers and mothers' nylon stockings and old sacking.

This is Vermuyden's land, the land he saved from the sea. The sea is now to the East and it's not very far away but at least the land here is mostly dry. This land still smells of the sea though, like it's never been away, even though no one can see it from here. There are coal fields to the West and everywhere iron casts are found in the soil. Water is all around. Dig a hole of any depth out here on the lowland and within no time it will fill with cold, crystal soft, glowing, sparkling water. Such is the height of the water table below the land. It's as if the sweat of the farmers has soaked into the land by all the stooking of corn and filling of pies and struggling and has somehow been retained.

As we drift along we come to more farms, more trimmed haystacks, more steam tractors and straw dollies. There's a sign wrote on cardboard tied to a tree;-

'Be wear. Lam's in't rowd.'

The farmers are gradually beginning to swing the tide in their favour with the use of technology but that very same technology threatens to destroy the natural order and with it their very existence.

Some are struggling in their efforts to chain more timber from the wildest land down on Paradise Lane. Normally this sort of work is done mainly in the darkest days of Winter but for some, with the wrong sort of land, this can be an all year round activity. We pass by the land called 'America' – a large field, so called because everything is on hand – water, sand, trees of every kind, delightful pasture. Children have planted many a cork there in the hope of getting a tree. None have grown yet but despite the passing of the years some still live in hope. The whistle filled forests glow gently hereabouts. Warm eggs sway aloft in the breeze of the Cathedral trees. This land is touched with nectar.

Children spend their time hunting for foxes but never catch any although there are more than enough to chase. They chase moorhens and rabbits too. There are hares in every field.

A popular game played amongst the children is to guess how many hares there'll be in the next field. The answer can be anything; one, two, three ... even half a dozen or more but it's hardly ever none. The same children pull 'tatties' from the fields and light fires to cook them. Some children even carry small jam-jars of butter around with them to use on the cooked potatoes. Some also carry knives and tin foil as well. They eat unripe fruit out of the orchards and build rafts to sail on the local ponds made out of tyres, empty oil drums, old pallets, and bits of old rope - skills which have passed on down through the generations. The natural beauty of youth and the pain of age mix easily in these times.

Each of the fields has a name and its very own personality known to most of the people in the village. 'Thumbrills' is famous for having an iron gate and being a good place to shoot at the end of the harvest as all the wild life gathers in the last remaining, ever dwindling stretch of corn still standing which is always harvested last, after all other fields for some unknown reason. It's probably just tradition; the way it's always been done, the way it always should be done.

'Sandpiece' is a good place for crickets and woodpeckers. 'Greenholme' is full of sweet water ponds to swim in which are mostly weed-free and 'Connigarth' has rabbits and the best rafting. Old cars are abandoned in many of the fields with petrol and the keys left in, just left for boys to take turns in, to learn how to drive. Some even have tracks marked out with straw bales and obstacles mostly made of pallets and logs so that children can learn to manoeuvre and reverse.

Doctor Silus is busy killing in the fields round these parts. He's blasting away with his twelve bore shot gun at anything that moves. When he isn't curing he's out here killing. Shooting is a common pass time out in the wilds of the countryside and seems necessary in order to maintain a farming presence against the abundance of nature. Most of what he kills will either be eaten, (wood pigeon, duck, pheasant, partridge) or if it's too small it'll be stuffed (song birds and the like) and put on display in large glass cases in the surgery as if it might otherwise escape.

Forward toward the buzz of the countryside, to the beat of time, thin men and swollen women are sweating to give birth to the food that will keep the nation fed, through all struggle and strife; droughts, floods, wars, disease. These people are largely ignored, largely taken for granted but they are all true heroes.

Some people in these parts are still living on subsistence farming. They live on what they grow, feeding themselves from their own fields, there's no money involved and no taxman. This is 'Third World' living really, medieval surfdom. Money is always tight of course, or non existent in some cases, but these are amongst some of the happiest of all people. They seem to relish the challenge and savour the victory. Their success is easy to measure by the fact that they are all still alive. Somehow they've survived – indeed they flourish. There are turf fires and butter churns and spinning wheels in these homes; there have to be. Donkey men, in a life of total love, at one with the land; draining, watering and irrigating and most of it by hand - a constant battle with nature; with the weather.

Success is meals to eat, warm clothes and a few treats. Failure is more misery and unimaginable hardship. There's no real welfare and precious little sympathy for failure, although people do help each other out in hardship with anonymous donations of occasional sacks of potatoes on their door step and less anonymous gifts of second hand clothes that some child or other has grown out of, which is not going to be 'passed down', usually because he or she is the last child in their household.

Irishmen work like mules, sweating into the land. Labourers; men and women, children and horses sweat on these fields. They are never afraid to say exactly what they think or feel, no matter who is put out by their words.

It's surprising what people will do to work blisters onto their hands and their hearts, all in the name of survival. Warm women do their best to keep their powder and lipstick straight as they struggle on the land alongside their men. To these people of the land, the land is often both the question and the answer.

Auntie Gladys is saving up for her boys for Christmas, so are most of the other ladies who are toiling on the land with her, but some are more secretive about it. Others try to make out that they don't really need the money...

Woman Land Worker1:

"My husband wouldn't be happy if he knew I was working."

They are all trying to survive the challenges of life and the dreadful curse of aspiration. Stories are told and re-told to confirm to each other what they are striving for.

Woman Land Worker2:

"No good Boyyo came to our house, midday it was on Christmas Day. They'd eaten their Christmas cake. 'Can I have some Christmas cake?' he said to our Lilac. 'No our Lilac,' I said, 'We're saving it for'd Show."

The village 'Show' is on the last Saturday in June. Not long to wait now. It is the most important high day of the year when farmers and market gardeners alike gather to roast an ox and show off their finest animals and their fruit and vegetables and the various products of their labours. The Show (t'Sharw) provides the chance for people of all walks of life to show off their talents. Ladies of the 'Women's Institute' compete with the finest wines and jams they have manufactured from the most unlikely of fruits and vegetation - nettles and carrots and elder flower - wine bottled and labelled and so very precious. For most people, this is the only wine they get to drink– few have ever tasted grape wines or even wanted to. Fat, herb sausages compete for attention in the Show against caged birds and exotic creatures and caged, finger biting ferrets – 'Howls and Hotters.'

The 'Show' is always packed with so many wonderful things to see, no wonder it is so eagerly anticipated - handicraft, woodwork, cakes, flowers, animals, sweets and sweats of every description; dogs, horses of all sizes and colours and patterns and types.

There's horse jumping for horses that can jump who are tended by people who are minded to make them and there's always a special attraction - something original. In years past there has been a rodeo, a man diving into a tub of flames, police dogs, Red Indians on motorbikes (although their authenticity was called in to question when it was discovered they all had Barnsley accents,) stock cars, stunt men of all kinds, even clowns. But this is Spring-time, the ox is still suckling on the bright grass and will do for a few more weeks as the year is still innocent.

Out on the fields two women discuss the prospect of a week at the seaside. Work brings them these kinds of possibilities. In these times, a holiday means only one place – the bleak Lincolnshire seaside and the ever freezing cold of the oily North Sea but it's a break from routine and a glimpse of another life, albeit a very brief glimpse.

All this life goes on simultaneously; no one waits their turn. They share the same breath, the same air between each other and the animals, the same food from the same fields, they hear the same scandals, the same gossip, the same excuses and share the same fears and ambitions and disappointments.

Having walked far enough into the wilderness we come across another pub, miles inland, which is known to locals as the 'Klondike.' It was built to serve as a hotel many years before, when there was prospecting for coal in the area. It served as a base for managers and engineers as large bore holes were sunk into the ground. Eventually, after many months the project was abandoned as unviable and the 'Klondike' was left behind as a permanent reminder of the folly. It seems strange that it survives, it being so far out of the village but it attracts people for that very reason. It has an added charm, the charm of something unusual, something out of place, having to try harder to survive because of its isolation and around this area, many people can sympathise with that.

P.J. Naughton

The Pig With One Bollock.

Just a few yards along from the Klondike stands the small holding of "Old Sarah," pig farmer, market gardener, spinster and local character. Most of her contemporaries are either retired or lying in the grave yard but Sarah doesn't really understand retirement and has no wish to pass over yet. She's recently bought herself a new boar pig from the cattle market in Toffee Town.

Passer-by:

"How's your pig Sarah?"

Sarah:

"It's goo'ing back?"

Passer-by:

"Why? Whatever's the matter?"

Sarah:

"Would you have a pig with only one bollock?"

Sarah doesn't have much luck. A few weeks ago, the dog from the Klondike crept round to Sarah's house one Sunday dinner and stole a leg of freshly roasted lamb from off her dining room table, just as she was in the kitchen getting the carving knife ready to slice it up. The dog turned up in the pub with the joint of lamb in his mouth. The landlord immediately realised what had happened and rather than face Sarah's wrath and not one to miss out on a sudden opportunity, he promptly sliced the joint up and hid it under a bar towel. Sarah couldn't understand what had happened to her lamb but called into the pub to find out if anybody had seen it. Of course everybody had but nobody let on.

Sarah:

"Has anybody seen my leg of lamb?"

Land Lord:

"Leg of lamb? You must have forgotten to collect it from the butcher."

Sarah:

"I never, it was cooked. I'd just fetched it out of the oven."

Land Lord:

"Are you sure you haven't eaten it?"

There was a good deal of smirking amongst the assembled throng. No one had the nerve to tell Sarah what had really happened to the joint and the Landlord passed a large plate of complimentary free roast lamb sandwiches around once she'd eventually given up and left the pub.

Just beyond Old Sarah's is the 'Planting', a long thin forest and to the left of this is the 'Bombing Ground.' This land was used as a practice area for young air force pilots to train how to drop bombs in the war. The farmers still regularly plough up live bombs in the area. Next to the 'Bombing Ground' is the 'prisoner of war' camp. Really the camp was nothing more than just a very large farm with lots of Nissen huts on it and need of a lot of labour.

The prisoners here in the war were allowed to walk down to the 'Klondike' each evening but they had to be back before 10:30pm which was the time for last orders, the time when the last drinks could be bought. This caused some resentment amongst the inmates but the authorities wanted to make sure that the locals enjoyed the last drink on their own. I guess it was just a way of showing the prisoners that they weren't totally free but in all respects they were treated well and responded in kind.

The Germans were good with the mending of the tractors. It was early days for mechanisation and the technical reliability of the early machinery wasn't good, so it was useful to have young men around with a flare for mechanical repairs. The Italians prisoners mostly grew cabbages and made ice cream. At the end of the war many of them stayed on which added still further to the rich and varied mix of cultures and traditions in the area.

This place is home to airmen, Irishmen, uncles and thieves, Poles, Welshman, Italians; all manner of persons displaced by the war.

Descendants of Romans, Vikings, the Dutch — people whose families have lived and breathed the land for centuries like only farmers can, young men, fast lovers, lovers of deceit exchanging gifts and secrets and joy and disappointment, both mixed and hidden, missed and misunderstood in the giant mixing pot — the cauldron of emotion that is, always has been and always will be, the core of this rural village community.

Uncle Alice lives here, adjacent to the camp. As a young lady Uncle Alice once bought four different coloured fizzy bottles of pop to drink on a picnic she had organised for a group of small children. People lived like this in the postscript years of the war. Families were extended by friends and became 'aunties' and 'uncles' although they often had no official relationships or family ties as such. It was all about making up families, filling in for people who had been lost or had lost loved ones or had forged ever lasting bonds in the terrible horrors of conflict.

Alice was keen for the picnic to turn out well. It was important that young people enjoyed the best times as well as they could after all the struggle, the endurance and the hard times they had experienced.

187

So it was that all the young children were all given their choice of drinks and refills.

Alice:

"Which pop do you want Frank?" and "What colour are you having Willie?"

At the end, when all the children had drunk their fill, there was just a half inch of pop left at the bottom of one of the bottles which young Alice polished off herself, the only drink she'd had all afternoon. Suddenly one of the kids burst into tears, roaring uncontrollably.

Uncle Alice:

"What on earth is the matter Melvin?"

Melvin:

"I didn't want me *Uncle* Alice to have any!"

So there it was, from that moment on, young Alice became known by everyone, far and wide as 'Uncle Alice'.

Beyond this point, past the prison camp, runs Charity drain which marks the very edge of the Isle. Looking beyond here, over the vast flat plain are the skies of Finningley, the aerodrome and the constant roar of Vulcan bombers. At least one Vulcan is always circling through the skies around the aerodrome; wheeling menacing and slow. Vulcans buzz day and night like distant flies, one constantly revving up, droning every minute of the day, night and day and night again; nuclear bombs boarded and ready to drop - two miles of concrete runway and from far off, the howl of a scramble from the V-force...

Air Force Officers:

"The Russians are coming!"

Graded Pigs

Quite a few of the farms on the far reaches of the village use their remote positions as reason good enough to breed and rear pigs. They don't feel so bad about the smell out here in the wilderness. There is always good demand for good quality pork meat and bacon and good money to be made from a plentiful supply to the shops. What's more, the food for the animals is free for the fetching. All the pubs and cafes keep dustbins especially for the disposal of scrap food – pigswill bins. Generally it's collected weekly - by the end of the week it's usually green over with mould - rotten swill, the snorkers love it.

Pigs are generally graded by age into sheds on their farms. The small shed at the foot of the hill holds the squealers up to twelve weeks. They are then moved into the second shed until their first birthday at which point they move on to the third shed. At twenty four months they are moved into the top shed where they spend their last few weeks whilst waiting for their destiny; their final inevitable appointment with the butcher.

Sly Derek is talking to Old Jack, both leaning on the main gate to 'Corner Farm.' They went to school together, all them many years ago.

Sly Derek:

"Yes boy, no doubt about it, we are definitely both in the top shed now. No doubt about that."

The pigs come out of their sheds from time to time and roam their respective pens in respective ignorance. They feed and grunt and lay contented in the sunshine; in this paradise; in showers of blossom and straw. Little do they know that some of the apples that come from the blossom about them will be cooked in their mouths before the year is out. Little do they know that some of them will end up lying in a tub of brine for six weeks before being sliced up and eaten, fried with eggs and wild mushrooms.

If you kept going onwards from here towards Finningley, you'd eventually come back to Toffee Town. There you'd see farmers with binder band around their waists holding up their trousers, red faced and red necked through ale and the weather, smelling of land and sweat and straw dust barns, selling cows, scattering chickens; chaos and straw; shouting and coughing, eggs, cough candy, little plates of cockles and whelks sold for six pence, with as much salt and vinegar in Toffee Town market as you want to shake on. Six pence and as much salt and vinegar as you can eat! Nearby, more live chickens reach from crates.

The price of cattle and the price of meat both dead and alive and the price of cattle feed is the main topic of conversation amongst the farmers on the market. This is organic farming before we'd heard the term, for there is no other way to farm in this time. Illegal people stand amongst the farmers, people from illegal towns, trading illegal dogs and dubious fillets of meat, all slipped ashore without proper papers. They are never any bother though - far from it. They are the ones who are most careful to watch their step and with good reason because getting caught would not prove a pleasant experience, they don't draw any attention to themselves, best to toe the line and keep their heads down, and take their profits and get out.

There's talk on the market that someone has been wiping their bottom with the bank notes again. The money surely never smelled that bad when it was printed.

Whistle Wood

17. Farrer's Lane

Farrer's Lane takes us back into the heart of the village. This is another green lane, full of more flowers and gypsies and absolute charm. Gypsies groom the margins of the hedgerows, looking for berries and lucky heather and wood to make pegs out of.

Pike, as big as young boys, are pulled from the drains. Love falls like rain onto this Latin ground. The honey buzz and nectared hum and the sweet fragrance of wild flowers, complete this perfection. There is a pollen drunk drip of honey hives. Contented old men, netted and methodical, amble between hives with lamp cans of smoke in this distant croft. It has a monastic feel. The warm rainbow glow of nectared flower, feeding the bees and ultimately feeding us, proves that there is pure contentment to be found. Mown grass rests dying, its mellow tobacco fragrance scents the air. A mist of lilac is swept by a gentle breeze. The warm mowers rest like Bibles at the end of a Sabbath day.

Honey sipping birds twitch and dart amongst the elder flowers. Spring lambs bleat in this gentle Spring time. This is more than compensation for all the mucky black, ice cold, howling mornings. The choral dawn whistled up from the green of the hedgerows.

From first touch of light, the great golden orb has risen silent high into the sky, the very crucible of warmth and life. The radiance of nature in all its glory, the lily, lilac and wild rose, the perfect buttercup. The glow of colour where delicate insects shelter; fragile, watered, precious, perfect. The scent of verdant nettle thriving amongst the naked brown thorns, nature celebrating and resplendent. Miracle heaped upon miracle. Herbs for taste and relief grow side by side. The word of dawn is most sacred amongst all the words that have ever been wrote. Families of the Earth and of the fields, move through the field hedges enjoying the wild rose, the corn flower and the song of the multitude of skylarks.

We pass by Pearling's land, well kempt and tidied. The sweetest walnuts are found here, so good that people don't wait for them to fall, they knock them off the trees with chunky sticks, hurled with all the might their gripped yellow fingers can muster.

A nearby farmer once lost two hundred pounds and his trousers around abouts here, a lot of money way back then. He was in the bushes with the weeks wages for all his men and a sweet young gypsy girl. She said that if anything was going to happen that he would have to take his trousers off. Once he had taken them off, she set off like a grey hound with the trousers and the money, never to be seen again. The old farmer was left to flag down a passing car from the shelter of the bushes, not an easy task with so few cars on the roads.

Whistle Wood

18. Commonside

Once back in the village we cut along Commonside. Miss Sedgwick, spinster of the parish, (detached, large aspidistra) lives here along with her bachelor brother Harold. They are anything but common, far from it. They possess the finest bone china, both cups and saucers. Harold has auburn hair and a full set of teeth at an age well past when most men have lost all such refinements. He is an autograph of hope, a beacon to eternal youth. They've certainly had an easy life. They had money passed down at an early age and have never needed or bothered to work.

Instead they spend their days in quiet contemplation, reading and listening to the radio. It's as if they have lived their entire lives in retirement. You can tell they have money by their possessions, ways and concerns but they don't flaunt it, indeed she darns his socks and elbows of his cardigans but even by day he burns light to read, even when it isn't dark. Not many can afford to do that in these times, only people of real substance.

Suddenly there is excitement about the village. Elvis has got his motorbike firing. The echo of the roar spreads across the village as he flashes down the hillside trailing flame. The ground shakes as he thunders by, backfiring and with all his engines roaring and spitting and the sound of a thousand screws and washers shaking and rattling and the sight of Elvis, clad head to toe in leather, flashes past, flames roaring a full twenty feet out of the back of his grotesque Frankenstein machine. Elvis is drawn and pale. His DA hairstyle (Ducks Arse parting down the back of his head) is ruffling in the breeze. He is hanging on for grim death. The Frankenstein motorbike is at last alive. These are the days before there had been any real mention of such a thing as a speed limit. You are only restricted by the laws of Physics, your nerve and the maximum performance of your engine (or in this case engines.)

Waldorf Butcher

The meat butcher is busy as ever, chopping and slashing to provide the village with the very finest meat. Meat is the essential staple diet. It is an essential part of the cycle of production. Farms need the strongest labour, labourers need the protein to graft. The farms produce the finest country meat which in turn means they get the finest pool of quality labour. It is a link which goes beyond economics. An Irish man with a sack bag is waiting to fill it with the freshly chopped dripping beef.

Meals

In these times there are so few fat people about yet people eat plenty and never do exercise; well at least they never go to a gym or anything, they don't have to. They walk and cycle almost everywhere and graft of course. There are few electric gadgets, most things have to be done using 'elbow grease'. The energy required to do all the chores means there are very few fat people.

People have to eat heartily just to get by, just to survive. A typical day's food for a typical working young man is as follows...

Breakfast number one, beans on toast eaten by the fire first thing.

Breakfast number two, taken out on the land twenty minutes after arriving– sandwiches and strong tea out of a flask, not much milk because it's already well below boiling.

Lunch is eaten at 11am and is sandwiches, tea and a piece of cake.

Dinner at 'haffe' twelve is usually egg and chips and a pile of bread and butter if eaten at home, otherwise it's more sandwiches and tea out on the land.

Afternoon break (brek) at 3pm is more sandwiches and tea. Sometimes a piece of cheese or a few biscuits eaten again, out on the land.

First tea, just a plate of chips is eaten about 5pm as soon as you arrive home.

Second tea (about 6:30pm eaten when the Dads arrive home) is the main meal of the day; usually roast beef, and Yorkshire puddings, roast potatoes, cabbage, carrots mashed in butter, fried onions and copious amounts of gravy.

Supper is sandwiches and crisps and an orange or banana taken in front of the fire at 8pm.

To keep you going through out the day there's a constant supply of Oxtail soup, crisps, chocolates, bags of sweets. This is the typical diet of a young lad out on the land but even boys at school have much the same diet. Girls tend to eat slightly less but just as regular. Food takes a goodly amount of people's wages but few people have fridges or freezers so it has to be fresh.

Most people have a "big shop" delivered weekly (Friday nights) then pick up bits through out the week to keep themselves going. The constant supply of vendors to the doorstep helps in this regard.

The heavy food bills mean most people have to know how to 'make do.' Making do can be fun when you don't have to but unchosen it can be the devil's paw itself. It helps that most people are in the same boat and there are plenty of older people with experience of surviving the worst rationings of the war.

Past the butcher's we come to old Dinah's cottage. Dinah is drawing heavily, as ever, on a Capstan full strength cigarette, intended for fighting navy personnel out on roaring oceans.

Passer-by:

"They'll kill you Dinah."

Dinah:

"The sooner the better."

Eventually we arrive back at Madge's shop, back to where we came into the village. There's still more to see. Back along the cobbles of the main street we turn left at the crossroads this time to take a look at the other side of the village.

Whistle Wood

19. Petrol And Curses.

Back at the crossroads the definition of the roads is less than clear. The road back to Toffee Town is clear enough but the green lane past the garage seems to move with the weather and the seasons and the access to the garage petrol station moves with it. There is always excitement here at the garage for children, free stickers from petrol and oil companies and metal badges from truck manufacturers, Dodge, Ford, Volvo and the like. Children know nothing of these organisations but the fact that they can give away free metal lapel badges speaks of massive organisations with sophistication and wealth and the energy and courage to innovate and deliver.

Remains of road accidents litter the precincts of the garage, there are abandoned and "written off" vehicles to sit in and pretend to drive and honk the horns and a sense of disbelief at the smashed windscreens and torn metal. It's a strange coming together of the full life cycle of motor vehicle transportation.

Some how it seems strange that the smashed up wrecks aren't hidden in some way in the way that death is usually hidden. There's a sense of tension as young men with oil and spanners, hair tussled, faces black with dirt and fumes and sweat, swear into engines. They hammer rust in spasms and pour oil into unlikely looking vehicles, striving to keep nuts tight on damaged threadbare rounded bolts. Metal is turned, sweated, pushed, pulled, picked, touched and polished. There's a smell of turbine and liquid fossil fuel and metal paint.

Customer:

"How much?

Fifty squid?

You've got to be joking."

Even people who are normally respectable can be heard to hiss biblical oaths in the precincts of the garage. You can feel the electricity in the air here abouts. Young men are expected to perform miracles on the tightest of budgets.

As we pass we hear Old Lofty busy explaining to the young mechanic that his "three-wheeler" car has "four-wheel" drive. The young man looks perplexed but Lofty is convinced – it's the tale he was told when he bought the car and for the price they're charging at the garage, (any price would be far too much,) he wants the job done right.

Whistle Wood

20. Jack The Giant Killer's Road.

The green lane which runs down past the side of the petrol garage is 'Jack the Giant Killer's lane.' Passing down here we soon get back inland, back to the heart of the wilderness. Men and women on these fields are struggling with the full force of nature in the bleak open harshness of this Lincolnshire Tundra. Heat, sand, flies and sand-flies and wind bear down and there's barely a hedge or a tree to shelter under to adjust to the burn and piercing inspection of nature's relentless probing and testing. It's gruelling, endless, relentless.

Later in the year when they start to cut the corn, the clouds of 'men-o-root' – the storm flies, will be more than enough to drive the strongest men mad out on these sands. Millions of the tiny flea-like beetles will crawl and wriggle through every ones' hair. Only those with true passion can survive out on this land. Here success is hard earned. Muscles are heaving, even horses strain in the battle to survive.

The land looks easy and free but it's deceiving. It is mainly loam sand but it is uneven, there are many patches of wetland and even in the dry places the ground can easily give way to a depth of a foot or more without warning. The lack of shelter makes it difficult land to farm.

The hedges are thin and patchy having been sucked dry by the sands and the slightest wind is enough to whip up the sand and bowl clouds of dust and seed across the Tundra. Sand storms are all too common and unpredictable. Some come out of no where. They can last for days or be gone in a matter of minutes. The sands are rich in fibre and warp, which is good for growing good crops but it's equally good for growing weeds and a huge effort has to be put in to keep the land clean.

The farmers and their labourers have to be equal to this struggle. For generations people have worked this land and they know they simply have to succeed. The consequence of failure is just too drastic to consider. This land drains energy out of the workers like it drains moisture out of the crops.

There are different prayers for rain, farmers pray it rains at night for a good crop and so as not to disrupt the tasks in hand; labourers pray for immediate rain hoping for a short day. Pay packets will suffer at the end of the week but the labourers are not thinking that far ahead, they are more focussed on surviving the daily harness of their toil. There is a sanctity about this sweat soaked land, worked and soaked as it has been for so many generations.

Drifts of the sandy land are frequently swept into the hedgerows but the labourers persevere to haul potatoes and carrots from the dirt to be cleaned and fed to the rich and poor alike. The test is never ending. Each day of the year the test is to repeat what has been done on that very day in the year previous and the outcome, the eventual crop, depends on the collective performances and the countless decisions to make the most of the weather that comes. The outcome is the wellbeing of the nation, the very food the nation lives on until the harvest comes again. A good harvest means good food but any failures inevitably mean shortages and higher prices.

These people work and work hard for what they receive. They know it isn't all that matters, the weather plays a major part in the outcome but it's the best they can do – at least all the hard work tips the odds of success in their favour. Without their hard work they know they would never succeed. The rest is up to God and fate.

Weeding, singling or striking as most call it; harvesting, draining and irrigation; hedging and fencing. Many of these tasks are not fully understood by all that practice them but they know they work and are essential to success and so they are repeated year after year, within exactly the right season, at a time whenever the weather permits. It's all a question of survival when it comes down to it.

And they know too that thunder follows the idle, they see it every day of their lives...

Old Adam:

"Aye, thunder always follows the idle. Best not to get struck down for failing to do your share."

It's a 'might as well get on with it' approach. They know there's no escape from the vortex of death but no point in courting the day when it has to be endured; better to graft and stave off that most awesome of appointments.

If you've never farmed then think how hard it is to cultivate just a few square feet of ground – to keep it turned and free of weeds and greenfly and wire worm and beetle. Now imagine trying to repeat that task on a massive scale, with nothing but your bare hands and a few blades from a plough and maybe a half crippled horse and a few rain sodden, half starved labourers to help you drag the blades through the heavy sodden clay of the fields or the deep sinking sands, all day long, each and every day for weeks on endless end, never certain whether there'll actually be anything to show for all your endeavours at the very end of it all.

At the end of 'Jack the Giant Killer's Lane' runs the Warpin Drain, (*Waa'rpin*) good for fishing, snaring rabbits and thick with reeds.

It is well known amongst country folk that electric storms follow the criss-cross rivers that draw them to the electric oceans. Storms stir these lands. These are battered lands but the Warp land, often subject to deliberate flooding, is rich with minerals and in good years produces superb crops. The floods are the key to success in these parts. Flood too often and the land becomes too boggy and lacks oxygen but leave it too long and it quickly reverts to pure sand and is good for nothing not even for growing carrots.

From generations back mothers have told their children about the existence of 'Water Dogs' down this lane. 'Water Dogs' are mythical creatures, invented to keep young children away from the danger of drowning in the river.

Mother:

"Take care! Keep well away from Jack the Giant Killer's Lane or the Water Dogs will get you!"

Most children in these parts have been brought up with the fear of the bite of the Water Dogs. Mostly it has worked. There are very few drownings but perhaps the story has carried too much credibility. Some men well into their eighties still fear the Water Dogs and have never set foot down this lane in their entire lives.

This lane is host to a spontaneous wealth of nature. Here nature seems to hold the upper hand. Old men trap along the banks of the river. Sacks full of wild rabbits, tied up, struggling, ready for the pot are carried home but despite the sack loads of life they take away, they make no real impression on nature's marvellous bounty. The river steams and glides through the mud banks, rich with fish and colour. Old men are lined up along the bank, most of them angling for pike. This isn't just about sport, a good catch will be taken home to be soaked in milk and will become a good supper. This is a land of rivers and tides. There's a constant struggle with water, drought, drainage, flood and food. 'New Holland' is well named. Eels and toads wallow in the margins and share the struggle for life.

Across on the other bank, the sand quarries rest along side this idle tributary to the Idle river. Lincolnshire threatens but generally lies still like a sleeping dog. This idle, Idle river eventually pours its heart out into the Trent, confessing like only a lover can. Ducks, pike, perch, sticklebacks, abandoned rafts, empty oil drums and pond weed are all pulled endlessly towards the brine of the ocean. Men from Trent Catchment, alive on the bank, doing what they were put on Earth to do, scything reeds along both sides of the river; dredging and keeping waterways free. They are hauling weed from the drain with an anchor and chain from the bank. No need to guild these lilies. This plant life is as strong as plaited rope.

The men pull and sweat and pile up mound after mound of weed and reeds by the side of the river but the river and the weeds and the reeds just respond in kind. Despite all their best efforts, the river men barely make an impression on the growth. It appears to grow faster than it is pulled out. Gulls wheel past laughing. The other animals present, the dogs and cows and dragonflies and fish all appear to share the joke.

But it's not about this month or this year, it's all about the long term, looking ahead, doing what's right. Fighting a war that you can not win but fighting it all the same. In a nearby meadow, a cow pasture, there's a row of freshly planted oak trees. They are small but they are prominent as there are few other trees or hedges out here on the Tundra. They will need to be looked after if they are to survive. The young trees are nourished and protected, cared for and respected and so too are the people who planted them. People admire this kind of thing. Everyone knows the young saplings will only grow about one inch every year even if they survive, no one who plants an oak tree can ever expect to benefit from it, or see it fully grown but plenty are planted. It's all about doing what's right. In a way it's all about doing a duty, paying respect to the unknown people who planted the oak trees for us to admire and in return planting trees for future generations to enjoy.

The meadow teams with wild flowers. The glow of dandelions is dazzling and perfect lapwing feathers are strewn about. Local children collect them by the dozen to slide into strips of corrugated cardboard to make the most authentic looking Indian head dresses.

At times the village looks more like the 'Little Big Horn' rather than a sleepy corner of North Lincolnshire.

Dragon flies and flutterbys drift by as if to mock the scything. The railway line follows the river on the other side and this is a favourite place for children to gather, just to the left of the footbridge, to wave at the steam trains.

A patch of sand where the fairy grass is always kept tightly cropped by the rabbits, surrounded by hare bells, provides the perfect vantage point. The drivers and the guards always wave back. Most of the time they also give a few strokes of the steam whistle. All sorts of trains pass by here - passenger trains carrying men with glasses reading out of heavy newspapers, coal trains, trains carrying pigs or wood. Some just pull empty carriages but they nearly all provide entertainment of one kind or another.

But most entertainment is provided once a year when the fair comes round at the end of June to coincide with the village show each year.

This is the very best place, about that time of year, to look out for any of the heavy fairground equipment being brought in by rail. The fairground is located in a cow pasture back at the top of 'Jack the Giant Killer's Lane.'

The Fairground

During May, the preparations for the annual fair begin in earnest. Children start to save their pocket money in time to get a nest egg together so there'll be plenty of goes on the rides. It's always a big day when the fair arrives each year. Children stand at the school gates to get the first view. Will it be 'the Waltzer' or 'the Octopus'? Sometimes they also send a 'Big Wheel'.

There is always a Rifle Range, Hoopla, Pick a Ticket with an odd number on it to win a teddy bear or a gonk, a 'Coconut Shy', 'Hook a Duck', toffee apples, candy floss and hot dogs with boiled onions and lashings of tomato sauce. It's the same routine every year - boys at the fairground pulling girls' hair and riding on the Waltzer until hotdogs come down their noses.

Whistle Wood

The fairground always smells of paint and onions and dogs and diesel fumes and electric lights and electricity .... and excitement.

21. Whistlewood School

It is May but the school room still smells of daffodils from Rogation, and ink and coke from the boiler and cherry red polish, which is not surprising as the dark brown leather lino is polished each and every school day, both morning and night by the hefty Mrs Grey, Irish school caretaker and mother of ten.

The day is beginning to fade now. The children are turning out at the end of their studies. Some dart out of the school gates as if they are on fire, off to play in stack yards or to play football or lark in the orchards.

Others linger, as if they could do the day again. Skipping ropes beat across the concrete, girls adjust their hair bands. Heads of fleas are carried back and forth in and out of the school gate each day like the tide. Now the tide is draining out, draining away. Some of the fleas have spent so long in the classroom they've even learnt their times-tables.

Girls are chanting...

Girls:

"Chinese, Pekinese, mucky knees and what are these?"

Children mostly laugh and frolic and skip by rhythmically. Cheeky Jenny walks more sombrely, holding the hand of her small sister Lilly.

Cheeky Jenny:

**"Our Lilly has filled her pants again.
Where's Mum?"**

Grandpa:

"She's run off with a black man."

Some of the children, high on sugar, share out the last of the day's sweets to add to their sugar rush. It's amazing there are any sweets left. Trades are made. Jammy Dodgers are swapped for sherbet, sherbet for humbugs, humbugs for mints, toffee for toffee.

Spare half pint bottles of milk, left over from absent children are opened and drained down by hefty, gorging boys who dribble and pant. The names of the absent and the reasons for their absences are recalled as their milk is consumed.

Boys push and pull each other by the shirt and the satchel. They trade stories each trying to outdo each other with knowledge of when Jack the Giant killer went to the school and where he used to live. Pinky Dawson, square snout, curly tail, squeals around the playground.

The smells of cooked cabbage and custard and used rubber plimsolls linger about the place. There's a fragrance of treacle, a smell of flowers, a smell of blossom and the smoke of coke boilers and knotted meat, meat with tits on thrown under the tables. A light rain begins to fall and the smells strengthen. No one complains of rain. These are country folk and they are all aware of the need. The wind, the rain, the clouds – they are all welcomed. The rain falls on the crops and the children. Both grow prodigiously

Past the school stands Wigelia cottage, home to Mrs Grey and just past that we reach the village hall. Old folks gather here. They've been holding a dance. There's always a dance on, every week day afternoon. The one's who can still move are showing off. Some of them, even some who can't walk, can still dance. Bones are creaking and hips are clicking, sometimes in time with the music. Others are jealous of this aged mobility. Bingo numbers are called amongst the least mobile. Others spit and moan and swap playing cards and recall their distant, younger days.

The generations of people have gathered here for as long as people can remember. It started out as a 'Reading Room' many generations ago when very few people could read but it played its part in providing a chance of an education before the first school room was built. Sunday school and evening classes are given from here and many people learnt to read and write in this room, sometimes even late in life.

The years bring more generations; generations of people, generations of farm animals, generations of rhizomes and hybrid crops. Somehow, honest country folk have managed to keep all this going in some kind of unbroken chain down the endless years, despite all the exceptions of weather, the wars and diseases and strife. We are all fortunate that they have managed this great achievement and continue to succeed because our very survival depends upon this unbroken chain of endeavour.

Whistle Wood

22. The Sabbath

This day is not a Sunday but as the day begins to come to an end and the day's toil is completed, we are reminded of the day of rest. For the livestock farmers, there is never an absolute day of rest of course, even on a Sunday the animals have to be fed and watered but on this special day, work is restricted to the essential minimum.

The village school acts as an ever present link to spirituality, deference and an ever present reminder of faith and the Sabbath. The school is part administered by the Church and further along from the school are many different Chapels. Many of the differences between these various houses of worship, have been lost in the mists of time but loyalties have been passed down through the generations and often for reasons for which the current generation of worshipers are not fully aware, some families will only patronise one particular Chapel although the differences between them now seem very subtle indeed and in some cases totally indiscernible.

It's hard to imagine that there was ever sufficient population in the village to keep so many places of worship going but someone clearly thought it was important to build them. It's as if every soul counted so much more way back when, far more than now. Even the Catholic missionary is present here, although there are very few Catholics. What must they have thought back in Rome to send a missionary? Did they think men in these parts were tied up in cooking pots by savages with bones through their noses? Religion has clearly been an important part of many lives in this area, down through the very many generations.

Some of the Pilgrim Fathers, the original Founders, were born and raised in nearby villages. It's hard to imagine the disquiet in these parts that would have caused these people to undertake such an enormously risky quest, to leave this paradise to travel so far across such treacherous seas, to lay the foundations for what became the most powerful country on Earth.

The Wesley family also originated from these parts and lived here throughout their lives. How did the teaching of Jesus make it from Palestine to this quiet out of the way place? It's amazing that more isn't known about something which clearly has been so important over such a long period of time. And why were people so passionate about their faith in these parts? Some of the preaching is very much 'Blood and Thunder.' Maybe it all just occurred by chance, or maybe fierce loyalties resulted from the influx of peoples from different parts or were the result of some other reason, now lost in time?

Whistle Wood

23. Back To Where We Started.

From the village hall it's but a short skip and a jump across the trod back across the 'Rock and Roll' field, back to the Joiners', just in time for tea and a few more pints. The men from the fields gradually roll back into the pub, arriving in twos and threes. The appearance of many of them betrays their trades. Some are covered in wood shavings, others gradually shed straw or brick dust. Gradually the pub fills and the smoke in the room thickens and the volume of gossip rises until it becomes a crescendo once more.

Outside, the village begins to wax. The sun glows as it sinks in the sky. Grey clouds slowly roll over the horizon. The fields begin to cloud. Even the blossom curls up ready for bed and takes rest now. Gradually the grey clouds become black until eventually the night is amongst us. Soon the nights will be at their shortest but immediately start to get longer again. By the end of the year the days will dim to little more than a glow, by then the sun will be little more than a stain but at the very lowest point comes the certainty of brighter days ahead.

So it is with each and every night. At the darkest point there is always the promise of better times ahead.

The lonely skeletal figure of the last farmer leaves the land. It really is too dark to see now. He flings his scope into a breaking trailer, along with a land blanket and a basket of potatoes for his tea. A chicken will be plucked, gutted and laid to rest in the black farm oven by his wife within ten minutes of him landing home and killing it.

24. Nightfall

People in this village live under different coloured roofs that look different by day, but here now, in the stillness of dusk, they slowly blend into one. Steam and smoke race from the chimneys. The unwashed who have never washed, once washed are as washed as those who have washed each and every day.

Behind the curtains, numbers are written and added and moved across the page - checked, agreed and disputed. The costs, the profit, the investment are all carefully weighed. Money for the coalman, the rent man, the milkman, the newspaper lady, the groceries, school dinners the red nosed clubman. Who will miss out this week?

Daisy Mowner:

"We missed the rent last week, better miss the coalman this week instead."

Candles flicker in nearly every window about the village.

The light of life which we are all part of but can never really understand, is gradually coming to rest. The owls slowly emerge from holes in trees and leafy hideaways and yawn. Our night is their morning. Somewhere out in the wilderness a lonely dog howls, amongst the smoke and loneliness. Mr Bruce-McDonald is shuffling down the street in his slippers. He's on his way back to the pub.

Mrs Beaver:

"Are you going to the pub in your slippers Mr Bruce-McDonald?"

Jock: (bellowing...)

"Never you mind where I'm going in my slippers. My wife dun't even know where I'm going in my slippers."

Mrs Beaver:

"I thought as if."

In the pub the ale is taken from the jugs for refreshment and is replaced as fast as the pumps will go. It's said that one Irish man and five of his work mates can keep one pump going all night, as soon as the last pint is pulled the first man is ready with his empty glass again. Men with fists of ale and minds of ale discuss the day. Men who have spent the day leading straw now lead ale. They've moved dust by the sack load and even more seed and pollen. The pub froths with beer and smoke. The farmers decide whether the last remnants of their grain will go for bread or beer whilst at the same time, out on the farms, pigeons, starlings and sparrows steal like rats and mice from the gradually shrinking granaries. Outside the pub door, teenage daughters with tight breasts wriggle past in their tights.

Out in the wilds, animals search for the last food of the day, food that will see them survive through out the long night. Pike dart as they hunt the shallows and swallow naive young fish which they bite and rip and chew.

Only the farm dogs bark now. Most are tied in their yards on rope. Cats fight and claw. Rats bite back but will be overcome. Spirits are alive in the streets.

Caster, Giro, Elvis, Tiger-Lilley, Zero, Pinkie's Dad, the newly married Dolly-Daydream and her husband, Pussy-Brown, Pog and the Three Wisemen all prop up the bar. Oscar and Dipsy Divers are there too. Mrs Keen Walters, with her piercing laughing eyes and easy smile is smiling. Even Sally Slack Cabbage is out and about although her perfume is not adequate to hide her smell of stale urine.

A young woman with no neck is standing outside the pub door necking. Eventually, when the floor is about four inches deep in beer, the revellers will float home on a tide of Guinness, home to slice bacon off the side of a hung pig, to fry it over apple timber logs, with warm bread made that very evening. Who knows, perhaps they'll also break some eggs or even some Guinness world records but it's very unlikely these will ever be recorded.

Sick children are goose greased and wrapped up tight in warm blankets with water bottles and teddy bears and liniment. By some miracle the vast majority of them will survive. In the morning they'll be given a cup of sherry with a raw egg cracked into it along with their breakfast to ward off the cold and ills.

The younger children hear stories of princesses. They've sipped warm milk, as slowly as they could, to delay their bed time as long as possible.

Billy and Bobby, piglet pets, have been fed with bottles of warm milk, wrapped in soft woollen blankets, kissed, cuddled and 'got down' in the Ramsays' kitchen.

Lanterns and candles are lit, books are read, children are kissed and flames are blown out. Dry oak log fires gradually fade in their grates. The glowing logs flicker and project magic images about the room as they play with the random light. Lanterns and paraffin lick their rooms with light and flame and fire and warmth. Trees lay slain, condemned without a word and without guilt. Still there is no blame than what the world believes, killed, felled, chopped, dried and now burnt.

But there is beauty and fragrance in this death. The sacrifice of the dead forest is not for nothing, it brings us our warmth. There is a strange mixture of guilt and admiration for the men who felled these trees.

The flames eventually flicker to a glow, to their greatest beauty. The jewelled embers glow their gentle warmth. High in the clear dark skies, myriad stars also flicker their wondrous beauty. Kisses are stolen. In the darkness there is already a fragrance of the dawn. Somewhere out in the ferment, a brand new child is born, arriving on this Earth, struggling through the pains of birth. A thousand Madonnas and the promise of constant love is radiating from the tea leaf stars.

Prayers are said, bribes are made, teeth are cleaned. Dusty books are read again. Some secrets have been kept another day, a world within a world. Death circles constantly, many are aware of this as they take to their beds but most people are too polite or too afraid to mention it.

Out in his coalhouse, Mr Beaver grins in triumph as he stands with a large rat clasped between his knees whilst he searches a rusty metal box for an appropriate implement to subdue the animal.

It is indeed a fortunate animal, to be caught by the very man whose livelihood relies on the very existence of this and other such animals. Any other man in the village would have stamped it into oblivion but to the paid rat catcher, these animals are pure money in the bank, to be nurtured and cared for. The lucky creature will later be revived and placed in a caged harem in the dead of night, where it will believe it has already died and arrived in heaven.

Deep in the fire grate of smallholder Toss Lester, the spirit of a pig ghost is materializing. A small group of people have gathered to witness the sight. The pig comes through the flames and appears in front of the fire most evenings whenever there is whisky in the house. Those present are amazed, although many have witnessed the ghost many times before.

Old Adam: (shouting...)
"Let's kill the pig, let's kill him dead."

The pig begins to squeal in clear distress.

Whistle Wood

Toss:

"Leave the pig alone, let him sleep, he's done no wrong."

Gradually the pig settles back to sleep and eventually its image fades away back into the smoke. Drugged by smoke fires, late night séances are conjured up from a pack of cards behind the thick, dark curtains of a remote cottage deep in land. The planchette of the Ouija is pulled and pushed but still the spirits won't admit that the object of Tattoo's affections will ever marry her.

Across the town, moon touched rainbow love descends. The rivers and fields, the flowers and the dreams all merge as one. The Idle river appears to slumber, as wild lily perfume poetry rises in the steam of the hedgerows around this land, this land of the Pilgrim Fathers, the land which they decided to forsake.

For this day the chores have all been completed. Tomorrow most of them will be repeated; hoeing, weeding, singling and striking - the land will be dug and turned once more. Later in the year there'll be corn to cut, apples to be picked, carrots to collect, beet to screw, berries and currants and peas to pick and mangles to heave out of the sodden Winter land. Acre upon acre of land and every square inch matters.

These farms are hives of endless industry, never ending cycles of toil of duty and stewardship and care. The chickens roost now in contentment having been fed, the lambs have all been brushed, the eggs that could be found have been collected and washed and are now lying in wait in the cool sculleries, ready to be broken into pans for the first makings of breakfast at the first strike of dawn.

Sleep comes now. Dreams are dreamt.

One-by-one the people of the village drift into their unconscious slumber, one by one they slip off into eternity, into their far off private spiritual lands.

They'll drift slowly through their paradise, floating in a half world, somewhere mysterious, floating suspended somewhere between life and death and in the morning they'll wake to a bright new dawn. The birds will be singing. The world will have finally turned once more. There'll be new flowers to smell, new nests in the hedgerows and more stories to be heard. Collectively by the morning the townsfolk will have the memory of another dream and together will have become yet another day wiser.

Dreams are lived out now, pure dreams untouched by reality, as the town slumbers, sharing breath not only with the others in the town but with the birds in the forest and the creatures in the farm yards and the beasts that lurk in the distant, far off, jungle forest lands.

For now the people are lost to sleep and lost to time. Young girls are lying in their beds, smelling of lambs' milk and rose buds and carefully combed hair and apple blossom; dreaming of wedding bells and prams - pure girls, some pure but no longer wanting to be.

Boys, smelling of dogs and butter, dream of fighting and throwing apples in the orchard and laugh cheekily in *their* sleep. They dream of growing up and owning cattle and cars and land and tractors.

The men folk smell of tobacco and dark, treacle black ale. They snore and dream of their youth and their romantic encounters. They dream of piracy and high drama.

And the women, drunk on exhaustion, dream of tidy children and tidy houses and romance and leisure and riches and fine clothes. They lie in shallow sleep, keeping an ear out for the sound of crying. They smell of fresh cooked bacon and pastry. They are too exhausted to dream of anything more.

Tomorrow the boys will fight in the orchards. One day the girls will get their wedding bells. Sadly few of the other dreams will ever come true. But still that does nothing to diminish the pleasure of the illusion, the happiness of the moments lost in oblivion.

Outside, wide eyed cats watch, alert. Their eyes glow as they savour the prospect of another night of hunting.

Rats waltz in the barns, spiders dance in beds. Couples couple and struggle and grunt in paradise. Nights are drawing towards the cusp of Summer. The believers are spinning in their beds and the revellers will spin too when they finally arrive at their rest.

Across the Trossocks, wolf dogs howl and threaten. These are wild dogs and their eyes betray their heritage.

Tomorrow the birds of the hedgerows will sing their hearts out in orchestral perfection but for now the village sleeps. Occasional mice slip as silent as they can into a granary or hen house in search of a few golden nuggets of corn. Dogs are now chained as a kaleidoscope of thoughts and deeds circles the collective minds of the village.

Out on the Turbary the ghost of a long dead ploughman trudges a slow ghostly furrow behind the ghost of a long dead cart horse. Somehow, even in death, they live on.

White owls flap silently into ghostly trees careful not to disturb the living dead. As other owls circle the land, mice scurry hoping to survive until day light. Cats howl and screech at the fulsome moon. The milk churns stand silent on the platform made from discarded railway sleepers by the gate of Home farm. Even the pumps in the Joiners' stand still now.

The morning is but a few short hours beyond the horizon. Come now. Sleep. Golden day break is already on its way.

Midnight dreams of flowers are lost somewhere out in the purple of the night but alas the Churchyard must still chime in heaven or we'd never reach our return. The soft, gentle, glowing, sparkling sands fall slowly but steadily from glass to Heavenly glass.

High up on Crook Hill, trees sway in the wind to accentuate the noise of the weather. On stormy wild nights the giant ash trees thrash and creak. The noise of the leaves heaving in the blackness is like the tide crashing onto the shore, the creaking of the heavy branches, reminiscent of masts yawning on the largest tall ships and full rigged tea clippers caught in a violent merciless storm a long way out at sea.

Couples couple once more, poking, grunting, rutting, breeding, tonguing, snogging - frothing, spilling and squirting. Some talk incessant in their sleep but the talk is mostly random and mostly unheard but somehow the conversation passes through the village.

Mrs Beaver: (asleep in her bed...)
"She's with their Jack."

Mabel:
(sleeping amongst the boxes in her shop...)
"He'll be giving her a right good seeing to."

The rest of the living world sleeps, at least as far as the ears can hear and the sleeping eyes can see, sharing some painless temporary death. The paradise tides of dreams recede, hopes and wishes are decked with blossom in the quiet sanctuary of the hot-water-bottle-heated-to-scalding-beds.

Strange how we meet so many people in our lives, they have nearly all slept within the last twenty four hours, yet throughout our lives we only ever see a few people sleeping.

Many of the village folk speak in their sleep but only in John Joseph's house is poetry recited,

John Joseph:
"In rainbow glow the tides recede,
the tides of dreams ebb and flow.
Decked with blossoms of nectared bloom,
dressed in the fragrant choral dawn,
lingering on the edge of death in that in-between."

The school ink lies still now in the schoolroom bottle. The treasures of the forest shiver, as do the dark leafed violets. Even the owls are back sleeping now in unbelievable large trunk holes somewhere deep in the dense forest shade for it is that part of the night when almost nothing moves. This is the very Eucharist of the night. In the hymn book chapels, the cushions rest in stillness. The village has almost vanished now in the swirl of darkness.

Outside in the yards, away from the dreams, the truth of life is hissing; cats yowl and spit. Flatland howling winds roll off the Lincolnshire coast. The axe-black howl of the 'recent-dead' keep people well below the sheets. People know people have been killed by less. Even the street lights seem to struggle silent in the stillness against the gloom and lonely bark of the night.

A wedding in the church is being prepared, in the mind of a young woman, but only in her dreams. She fingers the imaginary ring on her wedding finger. The Church is stooked with arm fulls of the most fragrant perfumed flora, touched and moved stem by stem in carefully dressed pots. There is the unmistakable sweet, honey buzz of nectared blossoms and the orchestral chorus tuned to perfection.

The honey tree hums softly in the chill glow of the forest. The silent golden orb begins each silent, magical climb from here, gifting light and gentle warmth to us all. At bridal light each floral bud will drip the honey dawn. Yes this is a dream but it is rooted firmly in reality.

The crucible creeps in silent rise across the chosen unseen arc, when alas, eventually to entice the dreamers back from paradise from where they must reluctantly return. As the focal dawn lands, love and hope collide. More dreams are brought back to the world, whatsoever love believes and can quarry from the darkness, whatever love can dream, whether thought or dreamed before.

The world has turned fully once more.

Whistle Wood

25. My Back Pages

Sweet sister Jane, God bless her, is out to marry the father of her child if only she could remember who he was. Then there's the woman she calls her sister. Sweet Debbie dreams of an imaginary African lover, imaginary for she has never met anyone from that far off continent. With all the lovers she's had, she might at least expect an easy birth. Trouble is she only ever had them in her dreams.

Mrs Wainright married a thief and found Jesus. James J. Ellis died a tranquil death and is lying contented in the graveyard, proof that there can be such a thing as a happy ending. Whiskey Davis is still swilling whiskey, usually in the Cumberland Hotel in Toffee Town and anywhere else that will still serve him. At least he keeps the dray men busy and will continue to do so whilst ever his liver holds out.

The Hardly-Deadwoods are still living in sin. Mr Grace died a most terrible death. He died before closing time. But at least he died like a soldier with his boots on like he always wanted. So many people were so badly affected by such cruel timing, especially as he hadn't even bought his round. At least he died the way he would have wanted, with a bit of change left in his pockets. Most people manage to hold out and die after closing time - at least it saves on any unpleasantness. They've always said that the Lord saves. Well he certainly did in the case of Mr Grace, given the size of that drinking circle. At least the vicar got it right – "*dearly* beloved." The regulars are mostly all still drinking in the Joiners'. Some are drinking to remember, but most are drinking to forget.

Stormy and Pot Roast suffered a very bad car accident. They were both very drunk. The police couldn't work out which one of them was at the wheel – neither of them it would seem.

Tight-Eyes still swears like a trooper and is still fighting. He's had his mouth washed out with carbolic, times without number but it still hasn't worked.

Mrs Browns favourite cat 'Toots' caught liver fluke but made a miraculous recovery. Dicksie went off to look for diamonds in the Yukon. Anton still receives a postcard from him at Christmas, when he remembers.

Old Adam:

"Has he made his fortune?"

Mabel:

"Well he's still looking if that's what you mean. Do you remember Ron?"

Old Adam:

"Of course I do. How is he? "

Mabel:

"Died a week last Thursday."

Old Adam:

"And what about his son Robert?"

Mabel:

"Been dead years. So unfortunate and what with their Kitty the way she is. His dogs still bark for him."

Mrs Cuckoo Bolton married one of the other Cuckoo ladies. They lived quite happily ever after, well as happily as charitable people can ever live. The inter-breeds are still thriving. Carrot's own sister is doubling up as his Grandmother and Auntie now. There's economies of scale there – it certainly saves on birthday cards.

Young Janice married a vegetarian. Their wedding breakfast didn't go down too well with her abattoir father, a life long one hundred percent, blood dripping carnivore with his extended canines and Neanderthal ways. He got a bowl of dripping salad leaves and a piece of warm cheese flan at the wedding breakfast. Gravy was still dripping from his gravy chin but alas it was from his evening meal of the previous day. None of this stopped him from handing over a brace of pheasants as a wedding gift.

Janice's Father:

"Salad? I want some'ats that's peeped over a bloody 'edge – a bit of 'jump-dyarke or some'ats. I do'ant want no rabbit food nor now't."

Most of the early beet have been lost in the heavy Spring rain. We'll feel it in the Winter when the prices go up. Gypsy Divers is still living at Hydrangea Cottage. The Gloved Dawson's moved out after being robbed. Mrs Duke Dawson won first prize for her strawberry sponge that her daughter really baked. It caused some gossip about the village.

The travellers are still here in number...

Gypsy Rover:

"Gypsy rover, Gypsy dawn,
wait for music, child born.
Gypsy mountain,
proud and brave.
Gypsy prayers,
men to save."

Sleepy Dawson found out he is related to George Washington but it hasn't stopped him telling lies. If anything he's worse. You'd think if he was related to a President, it'd be George W. Bush. He gave Dolly six of his best brown hens when she last got married. The shame of it!!!

This is still Tennyson land, "Ring out the old, ring in the new. Ring out the false, ring in the true."

Old Adam:

"So old is false and new is true?"

Mrs Beaver:

"How much more wrong could anyone be?"

But still the words of Tennyson endure.

Shearing is paying well – two bob a dozen but of course for that price you have to catch them first and that can take all morning. The red potatoes have done well on the strong land this year.

The three Sullivan brothers are in their very own race, this time it's a race for the grave. They bought a "three seater" plot in the grave yard but buried their father in there last year. He and his good Missus are probably still trying to find each other in the next life, probably trying even now to be more worthy, even though nobody was ever more worthy than them. His epitaph might not be an oak forest but it just might be an oak tree. He deserves that at least. He planted enough of them in his lifetime. No doubt they'll be recalling memories of life on the hill, the cool breeze and the taste of all that honey he got from all those hives.

Tango is still drowning in his own anxiety that no one else can perceive. I think he's beyond help now. There'll be a green ambulance turning up for him at his house before the years out if you ask me. I'm sure he'll end up in Lincoln. Nobody can do 'owt for him now. He's lived forty eight good years and six bad months. Some say its down to his breeding. Some say he's ended up with an unfortunate mix of blood - probably not mixed enough although he seems very mixed in his mind.

Digger, Sugarplumb and Geordy York are all dead. I hope we all meet again one day. Jack Daw is still stealing eggs. The Cuckoo twins have nearly grown.

Daisy's cat finally ran off. It was only to be expected. Perhaps someone will give her another kitten next Spring. There's a robin's nest in an old rusty kettle resting sideways in her hedge now. Some people just get all the luck!

*** THE END***

P.J. Naughton

Whistle Wood

P.J. Naughton

Whistle Wood